Praise for Bisto Award Winning
When Stars Stop Spinning
by Jane Mitchell

concept and conclusion are life-enhancing,
Ms Mitchell is to be congratulated for the
acy with which she paces her story and the
rage to have written it in the first place."
The Sunday Press

A tough, contemporary tale . . . "
The Sunday Press

D1589065

DIFFERENT LIVES

DIFFERENT LIVES

JANE MITCHELL

BEACON BOOKS

POOLBEG

Published in 1996
by Poolbeg Press Ltd
123 Baldoyle Industrial Estate
Dublin 13, Ireland

The moral right of the author has been asserted.

The Publishers gratefully acknowledge the support of The Arts Council.

A catalogue record for this book is available from the British Library.

ISBN 1 85371 507 7

Cover photograph by Mark Nixon
Cover design by Poolbeg Group Services Ltd
Set by Poolbeg Group Services Ltd in Goudy 11.5/14
Printed by The Guernsey Press Ltd,
Vale, Guernsey, Channel Islands.

A note on the Author

A graduate of Trinity College, Dublin, Jane Mitchell was awarded the Bisto Book of the Year Award in 1994 for her first novel, *When Stars Stop Spinning*. This book has subsequently been shortlisted for the 1995 RAI (Reading Association of Ireland) Book Award.

She has also written and illustrated a book for children in Irish, *An Loch Draiochta*. She is the Manager of Adult Services in the Central Remedial Clinic in Dublin.

To Gran and Grandad,
with very best wishes

PART ONE

Sarah shivered as she stood waiting at the entrance to her local train station. It had been the safest place to arrange the meeting, with little risk of bumping into anyone she knew. None of her family travelled by this route on their ways to work or school, so there was no chance that she'd meet with them as she stood alone.

Just to be sure, she had lifted her heavy rucksack and placed it behind a low wall, out of immediate view. Anyway, she was well off the main road, concealed by the lilacs and fuschia blossoms that grew in profusion in the little yard in front of the station. No one could see her there, yet she herself was able to see the road clearly. She could view the heavy flow of traffic heading into the city for work, but it wasn't the traffic moving towards town that Sarah concentrated on. She was watching the lighter flow that was heading south, towards Dún Laoghaire, towards the car ferry.

It was a cool, September morning, still, with a grey mist whispering over the glassy surface of the sea. The skin of the sea rippled where it was tickled. The air smelt damp and seaweedy. The strand was empty, but then Sarah didn't expect to see anyone out walking at that time – that had been part of the plan. It was important that her movements couldn't be easily traced. Anyone who did notice her from the road might easily mistake her for a commuter waiting for a lift to work.

Anyway, she had decided that if anyone *did* question her, she would just tell them straight out, no bones about it, that she was leaving home. So? Big deal. What could they do about it? They were hardly likely to grab her by the hair and drag her screaming back home. She had discovered from experience that if she told people straight out what she really thought about something, they tended not to ask any more, to back down and leave her alone. People didn't generally expect you to tell the truth directly, they preferred you to hedge around the subject, to answer diplomatically and thoughtfully. Not to answer honestly and upfront and truthfully. Her father was always reprimanding her for being too straight with people.

"It's not very polite or mannerly to answer questions so abruptly, Sarah," he would tell her. "You have too brusque a manner and, from someone as young as you, it comes across as cheeky and precocious."

Sarah argued with her father on that point. She didn't agree.

"I'm not being cheeky or precocious," she told him hotly. "I'm just answering with the truth. If people don't want to hear the truth, then they shouldn't ask the question. If I don't like the way somebody's hair is done, then I'll tell them I don't like it. There's no point being all nicey-nicey about the answer. I'm not going to say stuff like 'the important thing is that you're happy with it' or 'it's different, but it suits your face' or whatever."

Sarah trembled now, but couldn't decide whether it was from cold, or fear, or excitement. Perhaps it was a mix of all three. She wished that she'd left her denim jacket out of her rucksack, but knew it was way down at the bottom, beneath all her other belongings. She wasn't going to start looking for it now – it would turn out to be the precise moment that the truck showed up, and she would appear ill-prepared and scattered. So she stayed trembling, tucking her cold hands under her armpits and hunching her shoulders.

A small mongrel dog trotted into the little yard and began sniffing around, cocking his leg every so often. Idly, Sarah watched his movements. He made his way around to her and smelt the toe of her boot with interest, eyeing her suspiciously.

"Hiya, boy," Sarah muttered.

The little dog lost interest after a few moments and continued his morning amble, trotting across to the high ditch alongside the tracks. Sarah watched him until he moved out of sight. She took a deep breath. She looked at her watch. Ten past eight now. She'd been there almost fifteen minutes.

He'd said eight o'clock.

Sarah had been up before six that morning. Her alarm had been set for half past, but she had been so nervous and excited that she'd been awake nearly the whole night. Her bed was against the wall adjacent to her parents' room, which meant that Sarah had had to lie still all through the hot, restless night. Jumping around would have made it bang against the wall and undoubtedly her mother would have been in like a shot to see if Sarah was all right or if she was sickening for something, offering to get her a drink or to ring the school in the morning. She could do without that kind of attention, thank you very much.

By six, she had had enough and peeped out of her bedroom window. It was grey and quiet out on the street. Sarah pulled on her dressing-gown and went into the bathroom. She had hardly eaten any dinner the night before because her stomach felt as if a million butterflies were about to take flight all at once, but even so, she needed to use the toilet. It was nerves. They loosened the bowels.

Rush hour usually started in the Bailey household at seven and continued until half past eight. Everybody had their routines and everyone had to stick to them, or else there'd be general chaos. The big rush was on the bathroom, as there was only one to be shared among seven Baileys. But after years of practice, the routines dovetailed neatly together so ensuring that washes, showers, shaves and all else were managed by every Bailey in time.

Sarah's oldest brother, Mal, was always first in the bathroom because he went to the swimming club to train the junior swimmers at seven-thirty every week day.

As soon as he'd finished, it was the turn of Mr Bailey, who'd then pick Mal up from the club after training and drop him off to work on his way to the office.

Sister Alice floated in next and set up camp in the bathroom until Clem hollered for her to get out at eight. That's if Clem had an early lecture in college. If he didn't, it was the turn of Mrs Bailey. While she was in there, it was up to Sarah to get her little brother, Lee, out of bed and prop him against the bathroom door so that he was right there for her mother to grab when she opened the door to pull him in for a wash. There was usually a struggle with Lee who was like a ratbag in the morning.

Normally, Sarah was into the bathroom last as she had the latest start at school.

But at six that morning, there she was on the throne, convinced she'd managed to get ahead of rush hour.

Despite her optimism, the door handle started to rattle after a couple of moments.

"Who's in there?" Clem hissed from outside the door.

"It's me," Sarah replied indignantly. Could nobody even get a little peace in the bathroom at six a.m.?

"What're you doing?"

"I'm knitting an Aran jumper."

"What?"

"I'll be out in a minute, OK?"

"Well, hurry up, will you?"

When she came out, her brother Clem was hopping from one foot to the other on the landing.

"What are you doing up at this hour?" he demanded, his eyes puffed from sleep.

"Well, I could ask you the same question," Sarah rejoined, deftly changing the subject. Clem launched into an explanation.

"There's a crowd of us heading down to see the finals of the inter-college quiz in Cork university. We've to get the eight o'clock train from Heuston."

He yawned, rubbing his eyes.

"I won't be back till all hours tonight."

"Well, have a good time. I'll see you whenever so," Sarah replied as she walked into her bedroom and shut the door. She had tried to make it sound as casual as possible, as though it would be just very late that night when she'd see Clem. But the truth was that she didn't really know when she'd see him again, because by the time he got back from Cork, she knew she'd be well on her way to England and a very different life.

A different life – to Sarah, even the words sounded exciting, alluring, seductive. There was an edge of dark danger to the idea of a very different life that sent a shiver up her spine – mainly because Sarah had had absolutely no opportunity of experiencing anything other than utter safety in her entire sixteen years at home. Utter boredom, she called it. And she decided – many months ago – that she'd had enough of safety and predictability and a mundane, bland, plodding-along-in-the-same-old-way kind of existence. Life at home was a bore and Sarah had had enough of living with her boring, contented family. Everything about the Bailey household was so happy and balanced and normal that Sarah longed for a splash of danger, a hint of a thrill, a touch of scandal, a flash of excitement – just to jazz things up a little. There weren't even any old skeletons rattling around in the Bailey family cupboards to spice life up a bit.

"Anything that's risky and you can be guaranteed Sarah'll go for it," her mother had always said of her as a child – usually in a disapproving fashion, after Sarah had been fighting with the boys in the schoolyard or had fallen out of a tree or had jumped into the deep end of the pool before she knew how to swim.

It was a side to her character that Sarah was secretly proud of, that she relished and nurtured whenever she got the chance, although it was a struggle at times within the limits of her strait-laced home. She felt strangled at times by Clem and Lee and Mal and Alice and her parents – as if she went round wrapped up in a straitjacket labelled "Bailey" all the time. None of the rest of the family had her rebellious streak – they were all obedient and conservative and believed fervently in the traditional values and beliefs instilled in them by their attentive parents.

But not Sarah.

Sarah was different.

Had always been different.

Would always be different.

And now, she thought excitedly, hugging herself in anticipation, she was about to *live* her difference and was determined to make the most of it.

Sarah looked at her watch again. Twelve minutes past eight. Only two minutes since she had last looked at her watch, yet it felt like hours. He was over ten minutes late.

Sarah tried to push aside the frightening images that flashed into her mind. What if this Christy fellow had decided he wasn't going to go along with the plan as arranged? Maybe he wasn't so pushed on the idea of helping a sixteen-year-old to run away from home. Maybe he had let his better side argue against the ludicrous idea of transporting a mere young one to England, unknown to her parents. What if he'd called it all off? Perhaps he'd rung Karen and told her it was "no go"? Maybe Karen had phoned Sarah's mother and told her everything.

Sarah felt the panic rising in her throat. Her stomach churned. She kicked her foot against the old brick wall to take her mind off the possibility of everything going wrong. It couldn't all just fail now. Not after the weeks of planning and preparations, the scrimping and saving of every last penny, the stealthy packing of clean clothes and essential items. What would happen if it didn't work out for her?

Sarah realised – with a sinking sensation in her already delicate stomach – that she had never at any stage faced the real possibility of her departure not going smoothly, of plans turning sour and of her having to return home. Trying to conceive the scenes at home that she might have to face was beyond her imagination. She had only ever pictured herself arriving in London after a successful journey. Her mind refused to even entertain the idea of having to return to school and home. Even now that the thought popped unexpectedly into her head, her mind froze. It was all too awful and her imagination failed her – her thoughts unable to envisage anything but accomplishment.

She breathed deeply and forced herself to think positively. Karen wouldn't betray her like that. She was too close a friend. She'd have rung Sarah herself first. And why would Christy suddenly decide to abandon ship? He still had his delivery of batteries to make in Birmingham. He still had to travel to Leicester to collect crates of cooking oil. He had to get the ferry, whether or not Sarah was in the cab next to him. And anyway, he knew little or nothing about this young one, Sarah, that he was taking to England. He was hardly likely to suddenly decide not to take her along for no reason.

But Sarah knew that the plan was quite disorderly and that unsettled her. She liked things to be planned, to be properly organised. She liked being in control of a situation, but she had little control over this one. She was worked up enough about the whole thing without having a plan that she believed might fall through at any moment, but right now, there was little she could do about it.

Except wait.

Christy was Karen's brother's girlfriend's brother. He travelled regularly to the UK, Europe and further afield to distant places such as Thailand and India delivering and collecting goods for the trucking company he worked for. The previous year, he'd brought Karen's brother and his girlfriend to Germany for their holidays. It had only cost them a few pints at their local for Christy. Karen claimed that she was very *au fait* with the bold Christy and how to get to England for cheap, so she had organised it all through her brother. Sarah had provided the cash for a night on the town for Christy and that was it all settled – according to Karen. Christy'd pick Sarah up outside the train station at eight o'clock.

Now it was quarter past, and still no sign of him.

The hardest part about her departure so far had been that chance encounter with Clem outside the bathroom at six that morning. For no reason that she could understand, it suddenly hit Sarah then that she was leaving her family and her friends. And *really* leaving them – not just going off on a two-week jaunt to the country to stay with cousins. And not following some romantic old-fashioned notion about eloping, or escaping from a cruel stepmother, or trying to find a long-lost family treasure. This was for real. This was hard truth. She was actually going and she was not planning to come back.

11

After her casual comment to Clem, she had to shut her door very quickly in case he heard the sudden catch in her voice.

Sarah was very close to Clem. He was her favourite brother, even though it was with Mal that she had been in the swimming club for years. It wasn't so much the things that Clem and she did together, because truthfully, they didn't share that much in the way of activities. It was that they were always somehow close. There was less than eighteen months between them in age – Clem having only turned eighteen recently. They had the same views about a lot of things, and they always seemed to know instinctively what the other liked or didn't like. Like Sarah, Clem hated it if there were TV reports about whaling or cruelty to animals. They each also *loved* fried bananas with bacon for breakfast on a Sunday. Nobody else in the whole house liked fried bananas with bacon, but Clem and Sarah did.

As she walked into her room after saying goodbye, Sarah almost had second thoughts about leaving – just because she didn't know when she'd next share fried bananas and bacon with Clem. Her brother was suddenly very important to Sarah and being close to him was something equally important. But she'd resolved to leave, and leave she was going to do. It was all very well having a sentimental change of mind on the morning of departure, but she knew she had to stick to her guns – there was no going back now.

To get to the train station for eight, Sarah had to leave home before seven-thirty. Mal left at about twenty past, then there was a lull in departures until her father got the car out at eight-fifteen. Sarah would leave almost on Mal's heels, when everyone else was in the throes of rushing madly to get out of the house on time. She had stashed her rucksack in the bicycle-shed at the end of the garden the night before and she planned to leave by the rear gate that led to the laneway along the back of the houses on her road. Mal's and Lee's rooms looked on to the back garden and, as Mal would be gone and Lee would be sleep-sodden, she knew there would be little chance of being spotted while walking off with a packed rucksack. She had told her mother there was a class retreat that day in school, to explain her early departure and the absence of her school uniform.

At seven-fifteen, Sarah sat on her bed and took a look around her room. She had slept there for all of her life and it was as familiar to her as the freckles on the backs of her hands.

It had changed over the years to suit her as she grew, but there were reminders all round her of the different stages she went though as a baby, child and teenager.

On the floor beneath her rag-rug was the bleached stain where her mother had cleaned the carpet after Sarah had been sick as a toddler.

Sometimes, when the evening sunlight slanted in her window, it was possible to see the faint shadows of the teddy-bear wallpaper she'd had until she was six. Then her father painted her walls a soft buttery yellow, covering over the dancing teddies.

The miniature desk and bookshelf she had as an eight-year-old was now an ideal stand for her stereo and cassettes. In the corner stood the chest of drawers Sarah's mother had been given when Sarah was an infant. It had been a christening gift for storing snowy-white towelling nappies and scented baby powder and tiny hand-knitted cardigans. Originally it was pink, with stickers of babies floating in fluffy clouds on the front of the drawers. As the last in the Bailey line, Lee had inherited it, but when Sarah was ten, her father had taken it from Lee's room. He painted it a gentle yellow to match her walls and put bright yellow drawer handles on it and it was given pride of place back in Sarah's room for her winter jumpers, woolly tights and warm skirts. Last summer, she had brought the chest of drawers out into the garden one sunny afternoon and painted it matt black. She stencilled gold stars and silver moons around the drawers and put on brass drawer handles. Then she had lined the drawers with star-fish and sea-horse drawer-liners and now her chest of drawers was used to store her poems and diaries, personal letters and lingerie.

She smiled as she remembered her parents gasps of horror when they had seen the black and gold and silver chest of drawers sitting in the middle of the garden, drying.

"But why?" her mother had asked, walking round the piece of furniture and looking at it in shock. "What was wrong with it before?"

"Nothing," Sarah had insisted. "It's just better now."

Her father had stood in stunned silence for a long time. All he had managed to say eventually was, "But I thought you *liked* yellow."

Sarah sighed.

She couldn't linger long. Time was moving on and she had to leave. Outside of her room, she could hear footsteps pattering between the bathroom and the various bedrooms. Taking a sealed envelope from the pocket of her shirt, she placed it on the top of her chest of drawers. It was a brief note left for her parents, telling them she'd be in touch and not to worry about her. She knew it was really inadequate, but had decided that probably all notes like that were – even huge suicide letters that the person has sweated and tormented over for hours and hours. Who could say what ever makes a final goodbye message adequate?

The butterflies were ready to take flight in Sarah's stomach again as she made her way downstairs. She couldn't face breakfast. Stuffing an apple and a banana into her pocket, she shouted a "goodbye" up the stairs and, without waiting for a reply, quickly walked down the garden path to the bicycle-shed. Glancing back at the house, she unbolted the door and, in one movement, hoisted her rucksack out and dumped it at the far side of the shed, concealed from view. Locking the door again, she looked at her watch – seven-thirty-five. She was running late. Without further delay, she opened the gate to the lane, swung the rucksack on to her back and swiftly left without another glance back.

Now she stood alone and shivering, waiting for a stranger in his truck to collect her and drive her to Birmingham, from where she planned to travel on alone to London.

At eight-twenty, Sarah was about to leave her rucksack where it was and try to ring Karen from the nearest phone box when a deep-sounding horn beeped from further down the road. She scuttled out from the station yard on to the path and there, about a hundred yards down from where she stood, a large truck had pulled up on the kerb, its hazard-warning lights flashing. Sprinting back to her rucksack, Sarah gasped with relief as she swung the pack on to her back. She then ran as fast as she was able to the passenger door of the truck. It was already swinging open. To reach up to it, Sarah had to put down her pack and climb up two steps at the side of the cab. When she stuck her head in the door, a young man in jeans and a denim shirt grinned at her.

"Sorry I'm late – I got stuck at broken traffic lights at the Merrion gates. You are Sarah, aren't you?"

Sarah nodded, too relieved to speak.

"How's it going? I'm Christy," Christy replied to her nod, sticking out his hand. Sarah wasn't able to return the greeting as she was hanging on to the cab with both hands.

"I'll just get my bag and myself in first," she explained, finding her tongue at last.

Christy nodded.

"Swing it up there as far as you can and I'll grab it

and pull it in from this side," he said, leaning towards her door.

Once inside, Sarah swung the heavy door shut with a bang and introduced herself properly to Christy. They stored her rucksack in the space behind her seat. Christy started up the engine again, indicated right and pulled out into the traffic heading for the car ferry at Dún Laoghaire.

"It's a grand day for the crossing," he commented as Sarah looked across the still water.

She smiled briefly at him and nodded, but she was not thinking of the still water and of the easy crossing they'd have of it. She was feeling a peculiar mix of relief and a release of pent-up anxiety, tempered with thoughts that centred on home: thank goodness Christy had shown up; Karen was great to manage to fix it all up; would Lee have left for school yet? Would Clem have caught his train to Cork by now? Christy seemed a great person to travel to England with. Wonder what he's thinking of me?

Her family was busy with daily routines and regular lives, unaware that she had left, unaware that she had gone to another country, another place, another life. And, although she tried to imagine their reactions when they found her note, she could not. Her mind stopped at the point where they arrived home from school and work that evening, ready for dinner and a quiet night in front of the telly – everyone together, or so they thought – except that was not how it would be ever again.

Abruptly, they were at the ferry. After the formalities of showing tickets and verifying the truck's load, they bumped and jolted across the gangway on to the ship that was bound for Holyhead. The excitement of boarding and the business of going up on to the passenger deck and finding a seat jolted Sarah from her thoughts of home. She felt a sense of thrill that shivered up her spine as she stood on deck in the stiff breeze, watching Dún Laoghaire sliding further and further away from her. This was what she'd wanted for a long time now.

She'd finally left home for good.

Once they had arrived in Wales and passed through the customs at Holyhead, Christy steered the truck on to the coast road that skirted the Welsh mountains and they headed for Birmingham.

Gradually, as they drew away from the small stone villages and rural regions of Wales, the roads widened and became busy three-lane motorways full of teeming traffic. They hurtled along then, the truck swaying with the rhythm of the wheels, thundering past smaller and slower traffic.

Sarah sat up high in the cab, watching the changing countryside outside. The travelling made her tingle with excitement and she could hardly keep a broad grin off her face as she looked out. She was delighted to have got this far, to have left her other life behind her like some old skin that a growing snake discards when ready to stretch and expand – dry and shrivelled and desiccated.

Sarah felt ready to stretch and expand and grow. She was eager to leave her boring family life, to move on to something new and unexpected and exciting.

Her own life was too familiar to her.

Too predictable.

Too boring.

Sarah knew what her "planned-out life" in the security of her family home was going to be like, what her family expected of her. She had heard from them all about their values and beliefs so frequently that she was sometimes unable to separate clearly in her own mind what they wanted for her from what she wanted for herself. She wasn't sure anymore if her family's expectations – that she would go on to do her Leaving Cert, go to college, get a job, get married, have children – matched her own personal plans for her entire life.

She suspected strongly that they didn't.

"Education is the most important part of anyone's life," her father told her again and again – particularly after she flunked some school exam, or got a bad report where the teachers harped on and on about her giddy behaviour and lack of application. "You'll get nowhere in life without a sound education."

The rest of his family seemed to have taken his words on board and were applying themselves diligently to their studies – but not Sarah. She hated study and couldn't wait to leave school. She believed avidly in the wider education of life experience, not the narrow education of books and school and college.

"You're a bit younger than your years, Sarah," the headmistress of her school had told her, peering at her over the top of her glasses as Sarah sat in her office one afternoon following some misdemeanour. Sarah had tried to look suitably abashed and humble at her words. "Plenty of room for maturation in you yet, my dear. You need to think of yourself less, to look to your future, to become less egocentric. Do you know what that word means?

Well, look it up tonight. You need to grow some more. To reflect more on your life and where it's bringing you."

But that's what I've been doing for months now, Sarah wanted to scream at her. For ages and ages, I've been reflecting on my life and my future – and I have some ideas of my own. They just happen not to agree with yours.

But Sarah was wise enough not to be too honest and direct this time round.

The fruits of her reflection had been the decision to move miles away from her studious, conservative family. She needed to mature and develop elsewhere, to experience something different from school and college and exams, to vent her frustrations and apply her natural curiosity. She was well aware that the outcome of all her reflection didn't exactly match her teachers', or her parents' hopes – but it was *her* life after all, not theirs. Their ideas included even more schooling in the form of transition year after her Junior Cert, before moving on to to the Leaving Cert. Sarah couldn't stick that at all, and the family discussion of that decision had been the final catalyst that prompted her to finally leave.

She had tried talking to Clem about it, but he was more drugged by his parents' high ideas than she had given him credit for.

"I think the transition year in school would do you the world of good, Sarah," he told her happily. "You'll have a great time – work experience and project work and community involvement. I wish I'd had the chance like you do. Then you'll feel ready for the Leaving Cert and college after that."

Sarah scoffed at him. "Cop on, Clem. I know right well it's just a ruse to keep me on in school a little longer because Mum and Dad don't know what I want to do after school; they're trying to put off the inevitable as long as possible."

He'd been really surprised at her suspicious mind. "No, they're not. Where do you get these crazy ideas from? They just want the best for you. You must admit, you're not exactly the most diligent student in the world, are you? Another year might do wonders for you – give you a better start in university and all that."

Sarah had really given up on him at that stage. "Thanks a bunch, big brother," she sighed.

Finally, Sarah had decided that if she wanted to make her life her own, then she would have to get away from her family for a while. To live an alternative type of life not only sounded exciting and adventurous, but also seemed like a good way to step back from her own safe, predictable existence and look at it objectively.

Now she listened to Christy, driving along, as he told her about his regular trips to Britain and further afield to make deliveries and pick up cargo. And she liked what he told her about his lifestyle.

"I'm not boring you, am I?" he asked suddenly, interrupting her daydreams.

"Oh no," Sarah assured him, the anticipation of all she was hearing about and all she had to learn welling up inside of her. She felt acutely that she had missed out on so much living already.

"Oh, Christy," she burst out suddenly, "I won't have enough time to do all I want to do!"

He glanced at her sideways.

"What are you talking about? Enough time for what? Sure you're only a youngster. Haven't you your whole life ahead of you?"

Sarah shook her head. She didn't expect Christy to understand what she meant – at times she didn't understand herself.

"I mean, if it takes so long to educate yourself about the people of one tiny country like Wales or Scotland, how will I ever manage to learn enough about the whole of life?"

Christy looked at her, grinning.

"You'd want to slow down, young one, or you'll burn yourself out before you get beyond London. There's only you, you know. You can't take in enough knowledge to supply the whole staff of all the universities in the world. Just take it easy, follow your own instincts and you'll find your niche. Don't be getting all hassled now."

Sarah smiled at him. She wound down her window and let the strong breeze blow through her hair.

It had turned into a sunny afternoon and from the high cab, she could see green fields stretching away from her. In the distance she could just make out the murky outline of purple mountains.

She enjoyed chatting to Christy. He was a good listener, and an easy talker. The best thing about him, she thought, was that he didn't expect her to talk about herself all the time. He didn't probe and ask questions about why she was leaving home – whether there'd been an almighty fight with her parents or if she was pregnant or on drugs or anything. Sarah was glad of that, because if she had been giving a free ride halfway across another country to a teenager that she'd never met before, she knew she'd have been asking all sorts of questions about where she was going, and what she was doing, and why she was doing it and any other question she could think of. But Christy just listened if she started to chatter or chattered himself if she didn't.

Sarah shut the window and looked round the inside of Christy's cab. It was fascinating and kept her busy for ages, what with all the knick-knacks he had crammed into it. There was a calendar hanging from the sunvisor on the passenger side, and photographs of little children playing with a huge hairy dog stuck on the ceiling.

"My brothers and sisters with the family dog," he explained when he saw her looking up. "I only get to see them every few weeks, so I bring photos with me, to remind me what they look like."

Dangling beneath the mirror was a fluffy yellow mouse with blue stringy whiskers. It had turned kind of smokey-grey, which was hardly surprising because right underneath it was an ashtray jammed full of old butts.

A heap of well-thumbed maps and road-guides was on the dashboard. They slid and skittered across the width of the truck whenever they turned or swerved. At Christy's side, they fluttered and flapped from the breeze coming in his open window, but at Sarah's side, they just lay flat and dead until their next skate. They irritated Sarah. She hated it when something kept sliding or rattling or rustling or squeaking. At home, whenever Alice was waiting for the kettle to boil, or the toast to pop up, or just waiting for nothing, she started fiddling. Her favourite fiddle was the locket on the gold chain round her neck. She stood there, staring into space, sliding the little locket up and down, up and down the chain so that it made a zippy noise – zip, zip, zip, zip. Sarah could put up with it only for so long, then she'd blow her cool and let a roar at Alice, who was always so surprised, never having noticed the sound. It appeared that Christy was like that too.

The most amazing thing about his cab were the triangular side windows just behind the front seats. They had lace curtains – *lace* curtains – on them, tied with tiny silky ribbon tiebacks. To top it all, stuck to the window with a lump of Blu-Tack was a little plant-pot with a sick-looking cactus growing in it.

Sarah smiled to herself. It was pleasant sitting there in the cab humming through the countryside on her way to Birmingham and then on to London. She felt happy. The warmth of the cab in the sun and the swaying of the truck made her drowsy and her eyelids gradually slid closed.

She awoke as the truck jolted. Christy was manoeuvring it into a parking place at one of the motorway service stations.

"You hungry?" he asked, seeing that she was awake again.

Sarah yawned and stretched.

"Starving," she replied.

They made their way into the restaurant.

"How are we doing on mileage?" Sarah asked as they walked to one of the tables, bearing a tray full of food each.

"We're about sixty miles from Birmingham," said Christy. He looked at his watch. "Should be there before five-thirty if we don't run into any delays on the motorway."

"That's good going."

Christy nodded.

"Are you planning to travel straight on to London tonight?" he asked.

"I'm not sure yet. I don't know how long it takes to travel from Birmingham to London by train. If it means I'm not arriving in London until late, I'll stay overnight in Birmingham. What are your plans?"

"I'll drop you in the city and then deliver the batteries immediately. I don't want them in the truck overnight. I may drive out of the city a bit at that stage and stay in a smaller town – Birmingham is too industrial for me."

After they had eaten, Christy went for a short walk in the grassy area around the service station to stretch his legs. Sarah moseyed around the service station shop where she bought herself a pocket guide to central London. They were back on the road again within the hour.

As Christy had predicted, they arrived on the outskirts of Birmingham at quarter past five. He knew the city well and drove directly to New Street train station. He pulled in, switched on his hazard-warning lights and turned to Sarah.

"Well, here we are," he announced with a grin. "Departures and emigration, all rolled into one."

Sarah looked at him and smiled weakly, suddenly feeling very apprehensive. She swallowed, determined not to let him see that she was nervous.

"Right," she nodded, busying herself with dragging her rucksack from behind her seat until it was next to her. Hell, she hated this part. Saying goodbye to Christy was difficult, even though she'd only met him that morning. She was well and truly on her own after this.

"Can you manage?" he asked unperturbedly, picking a piece of food from his back teeth.

"Sure, no problem," Sarah replied, sounding much brighter than she felt. "I have to get used to hauling this thing around on my own, don't I?"

She climbed down and Christy passed her pack out to her. She propped it against the wheel of the truck before climbing back up and stretching out her hand to shake Christy's.

"Christy, thanks a million for the lift. It made getting here so easy for me – I really appreciate it."

He grasped her hand warmly.

"I enjoyed your company," he replied. "Whatever your reasons for coming over here, I hope everything works out for you. And don't get yourself too worked up about doing everything there is to do."

Sarah lowered herself down again and lifted her rucksack on to her back. Christy threw the truck into gear and with a brief wave, swung back out on to the road.

She stood alone again, as she had that morning, and watched the rear of the truck until it disappeared from view, then she turned and made her way into the station.

The station itself was busy – full of hot and bothered commuters who were rushing to get home before the half five rush hour – and, in doing so, were creating for themselves a whole new rush hour fifteen minutes ahead of everyone else. Most of them appeared to have season tickets of some sort, for they nearly all ran straight on to train platforms without queuing at kiosks.

Sarah herself queued at one of the information hatches in the "arrivals and departures" area of the large station. Taking a precautionary glance around her for any would-be pick-pockets, she unzipped her money belt and extracted a handful of pound coins. When she got to the top of the queue, she spoke through the microphone to the woman sitting behind a glass panel.

"What times are trains to London?"

"Euston?" the woman said.

"Pardon?" Sarah didn't understand what the woman meant.

"Is it Euston station you want to go to?"

Sarah nodded. "Yes, that's right."

She had no idea if Euston was the station she wanted to go to, but it sounded as good as any other. The woman punched some instructions on to her computer keyboard and read out the information from the screen.

"17.45; 18.15; 18.36 – operated by Northern London

Railways, not available Intercity; 19.15 and then at 15 minutes and 36 minutes past the hour every hour until 21.36. Last train departing at 22.50."

Sarah stared at her blankly, having only taken in a fraction of the information.

"Thank you," she said meekly. "How long does it take to get to London?"

"Arrival times – 19.29; 20.01; 20.51; 20.59. Last arrival into Euston 01.14," the woman rattled off in parrot fashion.

"Is all of that written down anywhere?" Sarah asked, knowing full well that this woman was not about to give her any practically useful information.

"Yes, here you are." She slid a small timetable card through the slot at the bottom of the glass panel.

What a ridiculous system, Sarah thought as she took the little card with relief. It would be far more sensible to have timetables to give out to those queuing for information and then just to answer specific individual queries, instead of rattling off a heap of mumbo-jumbo to everyone.

She moved to one side to study the timetable.

If she caught the 17.45 train, she'd arrive in London Euston at 19.29 – a journey of only an hour and three-quarters. It would still be bright when she arrived and she would easily find accommodation in a cheap hotel near the station for the night. She could afford a hotel for one night anyway. She bought her ticket and got on the train at platform 3, stowing her rucksack in the luggage rack.

The train was warm and Sarah found an empty seat next to the window just opposite her rucksack. She tucked herself into the corner and no sooner had the train picked up speed and moved into a steady rocking rhythm than she was sound asleep.

It was seven-thirty exactly when she stepped off the train and walked into the arrivals area of Euston station. It was a very busy station. There seemed to be hundreds of train platforms and roaring trains and people rushing everywhere and long queues for something and everything and announcements being made about departures and arrivals. There were shops and burger stands and photo kiosks all along one side of the station. There were black people and white people and Oriental people, Indians and Arabs and Hispanic people that stood or strolled or walked or trotted or ran in all directions. There were groups of foreign-looking people in funny hats and turbans, ticket-collectors and porters, flashing neon lights and notices and directions and advertisements that changed colours. The floor was covered with shiny tiles, and was cold and hard underfoot, so that women wearing high heels clicked across it, and little kids skated along next to their mothers. Sounds echoed round and round. The beginnings of announcements travelled right round and caught up with the ends of themselves so that only half messages were coherent. The diesel locomotives roared and trumpeted and snatches of conversation in different tongues and different accents tumbled in all directions, mingling together.

Sarah walked in a semi-stupor into the middle of this mad rush of life, plonked down her rucksack and just stared. She had got warm and sleepy in the train, but was now feeling shivery, confused, hungry and somewhat shellshocked by everything that was going on around her. She was suddenly very, very tired and millions of people appeared to be rushing at hundreds of miles an hour all round her. Suddenly, very sharply, Sarah felt her first pang of homesickness.

She wished she had her comforting, bossy mother next to her to grasp her cold hand and lead her to some safe haven. She wished she could step out on to the station steps and see her solid reliable father waiting for her in his battered Ford. She knew that he'd first beep the horn, and then get out of the car and wave frantically at her to make sure she saw him. And, as always happened, not only would Sarah manage to see him, but so would all the commuters entering or leaving the station so that Sarah always ended up with a red face as everyone turned to see who this stranger was waving at. She even wished scatty batty Alice was next to her. Alice would mutter some vague and empty remark like "Ooh, look at the people!" which so infuriated Sarah that she'd immediately want to get moving and do something rather than stand next to dreamy Alice.

But she knew her mother wasn't there to take her by the hand.

And she knew her father wasn't waiting at the station steps for her.

And she also knew that Alice was probably busy dreaming elsewhere at that precise moment.

Sarah shook herself and reprimanded herself severely.

"No one's here to look after you and lead you to a soft, warm bed for the night, Sarah Bailey, so get moving."

First things first, she decided. Some food in her stomach would warm her up. It would also set her up for a search for accommodation. Moving to the nearest burger bar, she ordered a large french fries, double cheeseburger and coke.

Within an hour, Sarah had secured herself a single room in a grotty little hotel no more than fifteen minutes walk from the station. She wasn't very comfortable with the ambience of the place – it looked very run-down and Sarah doubted if they got many guests at all. But she was tired and it was getting late.

Anyway, she promised herself, it was only for one night.

The proprietor was a fat man with greasy hair. He looked Italian or Greek. He wore a vest and had a tattoo of a naked mermaid on his upper arm. He smiled creepily at her. Sarah tried not to catch his eye.

"You staying for the whole night, love?" he queried.

Sarah looked at him.

"Of course," she replied. How long did he expect her to stay?

"You want clean towels then?" he queried, his hand lingering for a second too long on Sarah's wrist as he handed over her keys.

"No thanks," Sarah stammered, her face growing hot with embarrassment. "I have my own."

She felt awkward and nervous in front of this strange man who looked at her too closely. Grabbing her keys, she glanced at him briefly and went over to wait for the lift. He kept watching her – a broad smile on his fat face – while she waited for the doors to open.

"Sleep well," he called across when the lift finally arrived and she stepped inside. "Don't get lonely up there on your own."

Her room was on the fifth floor, at the rear of the hotel. At the third floor, the lift made a loud clanking noise and stopped with a shudder. Sarah looked around in alarm. She punched the fifth floor button again but the only reaction was a further shudder and a brief jolt. Then, the lift door slid open – still at the third floor. Rather than risk getting stuck and having to call the obnoxious proprietor for help, Sarah carried her pack the last two flights.

She was breathless when she arrived and her room was hot and airless. Sarah dumped her pack on the floor and opened the window. Then she moved over and sat on the double bed. It creaked wheezily and sank downwards at the centre.

She looked round the room. It was small and the lino on the floor was worn and patchy, but at least it was clean. In one corner was a small washhand basin with a large rust stain beneath the dripping tap, in the other, a chest of drawers with a wardrobe next to it.

When she looked out the open window, all she could see through the thickening light was a maze of alleys surrounded by high buildings. These looked like offices, their small yards full of steel bins, skips of junk and tiny carparks with only one or two cars in them. Through a few open windows, Sarah could see people silhouetted against their table lights as they worked at desks and computers. She looked at her watch – almost nine o'clock and they were still slogging away. Lit windows patterned the exteriors of most of the buildings.

She had planned to take a stroll around this area of the city on her first night, but now she was having second thoughts. That proprietor downstairs was some kind of weirdo and Sarah didn't fancy passing him going out and then coming back in later on. He'd probably have some sleazy remark to make to her. Anyway, whatever she felt about the hotel, it seemed to provide a kind of fragile security. After all, she had her own room with – she glanced at the door – a lock on the door. It was getting dark and she might easily get lost in the streets. She was tired after her long journey and her head ached. Maybe she'd just go straight to bed and get up fresh and early the next day.

Once she was in the bed, however, Sarah wasn't able to settle. She felt exhausted, but tossed and turned as if there were fleas between the sheets. First she was too hot, so she threw the duvet off. Then she was too cold, so she pulled it back up again. Then the traffic outside was too noisy. Then it was too silent and sinister. The tap made glugging noises. The boards outside her door creaked. The bed was lumpy. Her nightshirt itched. Nothing made her able to stay still in the bed long enough to drop off.

Finally, she decided she was thirsty. She groped her way through the dark to the washhand basin in the corner. On her way back from the sink, Sarah stopped to look out of the window, pulling back the curtains and leaning on the sill.

The offices were empty now, their lights out, their workers gone home. The buildings reared up – dark hulking forms on the night skyline, beyond which Sarah could glimpse more office buildings, and beyond them, more again. Occasionally, the angular outlines of the buildings were relieved by an archway, or a church spire that peeked out unexpectedly, incongruous among the modern office-blocks. The street lights twinkled below her, miniature white starbursts that spilt cold, blue puddles on the pavement. The alleys were devoid of traffic, still and silent, except for the occasional crash of a bin-lid or the miaow of a stalking cat. Further away, Sarah could hear the distant hum of traffic, the buzz of life.

Way up high, above her head, above the dark line of the buildings, a sliver of moon shone silvery-white. The sky surrounding it was stained milky. Looking up at it, Sarah suddenly thought of her father. He would have been home from work about six that evening, and was probably met by her distraught mother, clutching Sarah's farewell note.

Her father was a man of few words. He wouldn't have known what to say to her mother after he'd read the note, but it wouldn't have mattered, because she'd have had enough to say for both of them.

When Sarah was tiny, her father used to take her out into the back garden on starry nights in the summer and they'd lie down on the damp grass and look up at the stars. Sarah certainly knew nothing about them, and her father knew little more, but at a push, he could find *Orion* and the *Plough*, and if they were lucky – or maybe it was when the season was right, Sarah didn't know – they sometimes spotted *Cassiopaeia*. They might have found more had not her mother, always at the same moment in their stargazing, shrieked that they were both going to catch their deaths of pneumonia, complicated by piles and shingles, and they were to come in immediately – which they always did, somewhat sheepishly.

That night, standing on the bare lino floor of her room in the hotel, Sarah found herself straining to see the *Plough* and *Orion*. She knew in her heart that, whatever her father was up to that night, he would not be stargazing. Most likely he would be unable to sleep – like herself – and as her thoughts were filled with him, his would likewise be filled with her.

Sarah had been eager to get away from her family, but now, on her first night away from home, she found herself wishing her father was beside her so that they could both stargaze.

And when she went back to bed and finally dropped off to sleep, her dreams were filled with memories of times spent with her father.

Clem was dead ratty as he stalked up his road that same night. For a start, his college had done disastrously in the quiz. Not only had they come last, but they had come last with spectacular style. To make up for it, the team and its supporters had tried to drown their sorrows in the student bar of Cork University.

After a skinful of Guinnesses, which made them all feel immeasurably better, they had made their merry way to the train station to find that the last train had been cancelled due to engine trouble.

"There's buses being laid on for anyone travelling to Dublin," the porter explained helpfully.

So the bus it was.

Twenty-four of them clambered on to a boneshaker of a bus that rattled its way to Dublin. Clem had spent the entire marathon journey convinced that his Guinness was going to make a sudden reappearance, and the effort of breathing steadily and swallowing frequently during the drive had left him with a splitting headache.

Now, here he was at last, at one-fifteen, almost home. He was looking forward to his bed.

As he approached his home, he noticed with mild surprise that almost every light was switched on. The front porch light. The hall and landing light. The light in the sitting-room and in his parents' bedroom upstairs.

Clem knew his parents usually went off to bed around eleven, so why would they still be up? Maybe some friends had called.

He let himself in, squinting in the sudden brightness. As he shut the front door, the door of the sitting-room was wrenched open and Lee – pale-faced and clad only in his pyjamas – peered out.

"Lee? What are you doing up? It's one in the morning," Clem exclaimed.

Lee ignored him, speaking instead to others inside the room.

"No, it's only Clem home from Cork."

Clem followed him into the sitting-room and looked around.

His mother sat in her armchair beside the fireplace, her eyes red-rimmed and swollen, a wad of soggy tissues in her hand. On the arm of the same chair sat his father, who was as pale as Lee, his face grave, his arm resting around his wife's shoulder.

Alice sat on the sofa, staring at the carpet and absently twisting her hair into corkscrews that stuck out stupidly from her head when she released them. Mal stood with his back to the fireplace, his hands behind his back, a face like thunder on him. He rocked forwards and backwards on the balls of his feet. Little Lee scampered over and squirmed in beside Alice on the sofa, his big eyes fixed on Clem.

Clem froze, his stomach sinking. The blasted Guinness heaved again.

"What the hell's going on here?" he demanded.

Nobody replied at first.

"Will somebody tell me what's going on?" Clem was scared. He knew something serious had happened.

His mother responded with a loud woeful sob.

"OK, who's dead?" Clem blurted, fearing the worst. He could feel the blood draining from his face.

"Nobody's dead, Clem," Alice told him. "It's Sarah . . ."

"What about Sarah? Where is she? Has she had an accident?"

For the first time, Clem realised that Sarah wasn't sitting in the room with the rest of his bewildered family.

"She's run away," Mal told him, with a cynical lift of his voice at the end.

"What do you mean 'run away'?" Clem asked. "I was only talking to her this morning. She couldn't have run away – she said she'd see me later."

"Well, that obviously didn't stop her," Mal commented drily.

Clem sank into the other armchair, confused.

Lee took up the story. Too young yet to be as devastated as the rest of his family, one tiny part of him was enjoying this excitement, even though he knew he shouldn't be.

"Mum collected me from Seán's house on her way from work like she always does," he explained. "Sarah's usually home before us but there was no sign of her. She had some kind of holy thing in school today . . . "

"A retreat, she told me she had a retreat. If I could lay my hands on her now she'd need to retreat quick enough . . . " his mother interjected.

Lee went on " . . . so we thought maybe she was late because of it. Then we got worried when Dad and Mal arrived home and there was still no sign of Sarah."

Mal interrupted Lee and continued with the tale.

"I rang the school to find out what time this retreat was going on until because I'd have taken Dad's car over to the school to collect her, but the principal didn't know what I was talking about. Told me there was no retreat on in the school and, anyway, Sarah hadn't been in all day."

Alice felt this was maybe her cue, so she roused herself a bit.

"I got home just then and asked if anyone had looked in her room. After all, she might have been asleep in bed. Nobody had thought of looking. That happened me once when I was on that art course in Galway with Jasmine and Eliza – we were all supposed to . . . "

"Maybe just go on about Sarah, Alice," Clem suggested.

Alice smiled an apology.

"Her bed was empty when I looked, but propped on her chest of drawers was a note addressed to Mum and Dad."

"What did it say?"

Mr Bailey, who had been silent up to now, spoke up.

"Not much, son, just that she'd decided to up and leave and that we weren't to worry about her."

"What did she mean 'not to worry' – doesn't she

know I'll be sick with worry every waking moment from now on? All very well for that madam to blithely suggest that we don't worry and she off gallivanting God knows where," Mrs Bailey bewailed. "Anything could happen to her."

"Did she bring stuff with her?" Clem asked.

"Did she what?" Mal said. "Nicked my Swiss army knife."

Mrs Bailey glanced at him in annoyance.

"That's enough, Mal – you haven't used it since you were a Boy Scout. She took some clothes and a couple of towels and her savings book . . . I think that's about it."

"Did she take her passport?" Clem asked.

"Oh God, the passport. We never thought of the passport." Mrs Bailey cried.

"I'll check the passports and see if hers is gone," Clem replied, glad to have something to do that enabled him to leave the room where the tension was so brittle. His mother's voice floated after him as he softly shut the door.

"Oh God, if she's left the country, what'll we do . . . "

He was back within fifteen minutes, his face now as pale and drawn as the faces of the rest of his family. The news was not good and Clem didn't like delivering it. He stood just inside the door and focussed on his father's face.

"It's gone – Sarah's passport is gone."

Sarah opened the front door and walked into the lobby of the hotel. As usual, the greasy proprietor was sitting behind his desk, grinning lewdly at her over page three of his *Sun* newspaper. Sarah threw her eyes up to heaven as she turned to shut the door.

Here we go again, she thought to herself.

He didn't cause her as much embarrassment now as when she had first arrived. After the first couple of days, she had got used to his leering and his fumbling attempts to stroke her wrist when he handed over the keys to her room. She had been scared at first in case he tried to grab her or something. For the first three nights, she had placed a chair against the locked door of her room, but nothing ever happened. He just seemed to get a thrill out of touching her arm and smirking at her, or making the occasional suggestive comment. Now, she was just sick of the sight of him, with his fat face that shone with sweat and his hairy armpits.

By the time she got to his desk, he had her keys off the hook and was holding them out.

"Thanks," Sarah muttered, plucking them deftly from his outstretched hand with her finger and thumb, scarcely brushing his sweaty palm.

"I changed your bed-linen today for you," he murmured.

"Great," Sarah replied as she waited for the lift, ignoring his suggestive tone of voice.

The lift cranked its unsteady way to the third floor as usual, from where Sarah trudged the last two flights to her own room. Panting, she threw herself on the bed and gazed upwards, her eyes focusing on the large, brown stain on the ceiling.

She knew every inch of that stain by now, having stared at it for hours in the evenings after her days' ramblings.

Or when she wasn't able to sleep.

It was quite often nowadays that sleep evaded her, and it disturbed her. It disturbed her because she knew she wasn't completely at ease with everything. Whenever Sarah had a problem preying on her mind – a squabble with Clem, or a low mark in a school exam – it would gnaw at her and deny her sleep. She hadn't been able to sleep for several nights before leaving home, but she had put it down to anticipation, apprehension, nerves. She thought when she finally left home and arrived in London she would sleep like a baby, relaxed and happy.

But it wasn't like that. She tossed and turned most nights, gazing for hours at the ceiling, waiting for the floating, semiconscious state that always preceded her deep sleep. Or, if she was really fretful and restless, she would stand at the window looking out at the stars or smudges of cloud until she felt calmer and able to return to bed. Inevitably, she would finally drop off as the first cold grey of dawn began to creep into the dark sky, only to wake to her alarm clock a couple of hours later, feeling ragged and cheated.

Now, in the early evening, she stared at the familiar brown stain that occupied so much of her nights. Sometimes, she could see the outline of Dublin bay on the left side of the stain – albeit Dublin bay with a very lopsided Howth peninsula. Then, if she squinted her eyes a bit and twisted her head to the right, she could make out the shape of Kippure mountain as seen through a fog or low cloud. She had to add in that it was "as seen through a fog or low cloud" because otherwise, even with her active imagination, it was difficult to picture the great Kippure in the stain on the ceiling of her little hotel room in the centre of London.

Sarah was tired, but tonight she felt a sense of jubilation. For the past five days, she had trudged round every little flat and bed-sit in inner London, following up on dozens of ads in local newspapers, trying to find somewhere to live. Staying in the hotel – even though it was relatively cheap – meant that she was living way beyond her budget. The past few days had eaten a considerable hole into her meagre resources. She had been eating out most of the time – a luxury by all accounts – because there were no facilities for cooking for herself. Even the cost of a MacDonalds burger and french fries mounted up if you were eating them every night. She also knew that she couldn't start working until she had somewhere to stay and so it was with a sense of urgency that she searched for her new home each day. She had seen flats of all shapes and sizes, from luxurious penthouse suites, in which she felt a fraud as she tiptoed around in her Docs and jeans, to one-roomed pigsties where the carpets were stained with chicken biryani and pockmarked with cigarette burns, and where screaming children and arguing families could be heard and smelt through damp, paper-thin walls as they cooked their foods and lived their lives. She had been getting really concerned about not being able to find a place to rent, anxious about her money running out. That was probably what stole her sleep from her as she worried and fretted.

But today her luck had changed.

London was a massive place. Sarah knew from trips there as a child and from TV and school that it was enormous, but it was only when she was immersed into the midst of the pulsating mass of buildings and people that she began to appreciate what "enormous" actually meant. Everywhere she went, by whatever mode of transport, at whatever time of day, people were crammed together. The whole city was like the bargain basement of Clerys during the January sales.

And it spread out so, so far in so, so many directions. She could travel for hours and hours from her hotel room in any direction and still be in London, with even more and more of London to travel through before she would escape the city. She tried to picture the layout of the city from a bird's-eye view with her room at the centre of the imaginary map. But even though she soared higher and higher in her imagination, her mind was not able to visualise the entire span. She travelled so high that her view was spoiled by the high clouds and the mistiness of the atmosphere, and her eyes didn't have the width of field of vision they required. And still the city spread out and out.

She never went out without having her pocket guide to central London in her back pocket. She found the nearest underground train station to where she was staying. It didn't take her long to discover that most of the centre of London lay to the south of where she was staying, and so getting the tube into Tottenham Court Road or Piccadilly Circus was the best. She would squash on in the morning with the best of them, pushing and grunting and cramming herself in to ensure a place on the train before the door closed automatically and everyone could breathe again. At the next station, most of those just inside the doorway would have to unload to let out the travellers who were further inside the train. Once those who wished to get out had disembarked, the entire squeezing-on process would begin all over again. At Piccadilly or Tottenham Court Road, Sarah would then pick up her connection that took her to wherever she was going that particular morning.

Sarah hated the tube. Right from the time she was very small and her dad took them to London, she had felt a sense of rising panic. She hated the long, long escalators that swallowed up everyone who went on them and went way underground to where the blind trains trundled and hurtled around in dark tunnels. The trains reminded her of sinister overgrown rats scurrying around in their lairs. While her father bought the tickets for everyone, Sarah would stand in awe beside her brothers and sister watching as dozens and dozens of people calmly stepped on to the escalators and vanished into a huge black chasm, the very chasm into which Sarah herself was soon to go. Now, she was beyond that childish and irrational fear of being engulfed by a huge blackness, but her maturity didn't prevent the apprehension she sensed as she stepped on to the moving stairway and was carried deeper and deeper into the earth.

She preferred the bus by far, where she could sit up top and swing along above the crowds, viewing the city and its people from her vantage point. The only problem with the bus was that she never knew exactly where she was. While she loved the sensation of travelling way above ground, she was always worried that she would miss her stop and end up in some wayout suburb, lost in a mass of buildings and swarming people with no means of escape. The city landmarks meant nothing to her as a stranger and were merely more buildings or statues or parks. Range couldn't be easily gauged in heavy traffic where time did not relate to distance travelled, and the bus didn't stop at every designated place, so bus stops couldn't be counted or noted.

And so, for most of the time, Sarah used the tube. She could follow its route on her little map and know that when she emerged from the ground, she would be exactly where she wanted to be and nowhere else. The tube also meant that she arrived on time for viewings and appointments with landlords and owners as it was so frequent and unaffected by broken traffic lights and traffic jams.

Each evening, Sarah would buy the paper at the shop just outside the station and she would pore over the "Flat and Bed-sits to Rent" section, circling possibilities. Jotting down telephone numbers, she would trot down to the phone in the lobby. There, she would phone in advance and arrange to view the house, flat or bed-sit advertised.

Sarah had met all types of people showing all types of

flats in her few days searching. She was shown around by Chinese and Oriental people who refused to look her in the eye when she asked about the cost of rent and who anxiously followed her from room to room, touching and rearranging chairs and ornaments all the while.

She had met Pakistanis and Asians whose clothes and rooms had a distinctive, yet not unpleasant, smell of spices and oils and sweat.

The Greek who had shown her a two-roomed flat right next to the tube station had shouted at her all the time, even though she was standing right beside him. He walked ahead of her and threw himself down on the sofa in the sitting-room, putting his enormous feet up on a little coffee-table that wobbled precariously. Then he shouted to her about the room and the rent, the electricity bill and the rules for tenants, as though she was standing on the other side of the street.

Sarah had disliked him at first. She thought him rude and ill-mannered, but after a while, she realised that he was just a shouting type of person who was all blustery, but quite OK underneath. She had been about to accept his flat when the front door to the house opened and in had walked his wife and three tall children. They all lived upstairs, he explained. He introduced them to Sarah and to her dismay, they all bellowed Greek greetings to her as they hugged her in welcome. Sarah felt her eardrums were about to burst, what with five Greeks all yelling at her. There was no way she could stick it long-term and so, regretfully, she decided not to take the room, although the price was good.

Finally, she went to see a small bed-sit in a high, red-bricked house near the centre of the city. The ad for it had been small and unobtrusive, only two lines long, which Sarah almost missed: "One room, with cooking facilities and toilet. Close to the city, cheap rent." The phone number was local. There was no name.

When she called, the phone had rung for a long, long time before being answered, but the woman she spoke to sounded gentle. Sarah arranged to call there the following afternoon at four o'clock. The woman gave her careful directions.

It was five to four when Sarah climbed the granite steps to the house and knocked. A small woman carrying a tiny child opened the door and introduced herself as Mrs Afandi. She wore a brilliant pink sari stitched with sequins that shimmered and rattled softly as she walked. Mrs Afandi brought Sarah up three flights of stairs and unlocked the door to the room.

They stepped inside and Sarah looked around.

The room was small and square, the walls painted a colour that at one time must have been cream but now was a variegated shade of grey. Opposite the door was a window, beneath which was a sagging sofa with a kitchen table in front of it.

"Do you like the room?" asked Mrs Afandi softly. She fixed Sarah with anxious brown eyes.

Sarah smiled at her. She looked round the room again.

"Where can I cook?" she enquired, not responding directly to the question asked.

"Over here."

Mrs Afandi led the way to the far side of the room next to the window, where a small worktop area with a sink and a two-ring stove was cunningly concealed behind a screen. The rings were filthy: caked with baked-on dirt that was charred black. There was a dead busy-lizzie, a motionless upside-down bluebottle and a scorched geranium on the windowsill. Opening one of the two cupboards, Sarah recoiled from the sight of mouse droppings behind a furred jar of jam, but she forced herself to swallow her pride and high expectations. Beggars can't be choosers and at the rate her home-search was going, she would soon be a beggar. Nothing a good dose of Dettol and a bit of elbow-grease won't clean up, she told herself. And a few cheap mouse-traps will soon move any unwelcome guests.

Mrs Afandi piped up from behind her.

"My sons will clean all this for you. They will scrub and wash and wipe. They are good workers and this room will be like new for you. You like it? All the furniture is for your use." Mrs Afandi generously indicated the sagging sofa, the stained kitchen table and the bed against the wall.

Looking round her, Sarah nodded cautiously, enquiring,

"Can I see the bathroom?"

Mrs Afandi's eyes lowered apologetically. She shook her head.

"No, no. No bathroom – ad only said toilet. Shower is across the hall, shared between four rooms. Your toilet is here."

She scuttled across to a small doorway behind the main door of the room and opened it. There was a toilet and tiny washhand basin.

At least she didn't have to share a toilet. And a

shower between only four was fine. After all, at home she was used to sharing a shower with six others.

Leaving Mrs Afandi that afternoon, Sarah felt happy. She had her own room with washing and cooking facilities and a private loo. She had arranged with Mrs Afandi that her sons would wash and clean and scrub the kitchen and toilet area. They would also vacuum the floor and polish the windows, and set mouse-traps which Mrs Afandi assured Sarah would be emptied for her.

The room would be ready from six o'clock the following evening, and Sarah had paid Mrs Afandi six weeks rent in advance. Her rent covered lighting and cooking, and there was a pay-phone in the entrance lobby. She had to look after her own heating, but there was a meter-operated heater in the room.

That evening, Sarah lay on her hotel bed and stared at her stain, knowing that tomorrow evening she would be busy sorting out her own belongings in her new little flat. She would be far away from the greasy leering proprietor downstairs, and she could begin to build her new life and decide herself what direction it was going to take.

Even though she was delighted, Sarah was also aware of a niggling little worry at the back of her mind. In fact, there were two niggling little worries at the back of her mind.

The first was money. She had given to Mrs Afandi almost all that she had in order to pay her the rent in advance. That was part of the agreement, but now Sarah had only enough money to last her for a few days – and even that was if she lived very frugally. With virtually no money in her pocket, it was essential that she secure some kind of job for herself almost immediately. It worried her. Because it had taken her over a week to find accommodation, it might also take her a week to find a job, and she knew that she had nothing like enough money to last her for over a week. The one good thing was that she didn't owe the hotel anything because she had paid for each night in advance – the proprietor wouldn't have it any other way – so she had no bills to worry about.

Sarah was also worried about her family. She was worried that her dad's ulcer might have flared up with all the stress, and she worried about little Lee and Clem. She wanted to ring and talk to them. She wanted to tell them that she was well and happy, that she had found a flat of her own and that London was exciting and that she was glad she had travelled over. She wanted them to tell her how they loved her and how they knew she had made the right decision after all about her life.

But Sarah knew that she could not ring them. She knew that she would only drive them frantic with worry and sick with anxiety. They would not believe that she was happy and well. They would want to send her money and plane tickets. They would want to come and collect her and bring her back home to the warm family. Most of all, she knew that they would not tell her that she had made the right decision about her life. They would tell her that what she was doing was foolish and silly and dangerous.

And Sarah did not want to hear those words. She was not ready to be told things like that.

The six Afandi children thundering downstairs on their way to school woke Sarah in the morning without fail. Without having to look at her watch, she knew it was ten past eight.

At ten past eight every morning, Mrs Afandi accompanied her six wild children with their round eyes and black, black hair to school. She would open the door upstairs and they would clatter down the four flights of stairs from their two-room home to the street below, while she stood on the top step and implored them to go quietly and slowly.

Sarah lay in her narrow little bed after stretching and sleepily looked at the light that hung from a black frayed cord in the centre of the room. If she watched very carefully, she was able to see the bulb drift gently to and fro from the vibrations of twelve little feet on the wooden stairs of the house. A couple of moments later, Mrs Afandi herself – carrying her seventh and youngest child – would make her way down to the street where her children waited for her.

Sarah yawned and sat up, urging herself to get ready for work. She had to be at the deli at twenty to nine to take the lunch orders for the day from the commuters who worked in the area. She always left herself barely enough time to get there and she knew that Bakhtiar would be narked if she was late because then he would have to take all the orders himself.

Not that it was too difficult a job for him to do on his own, Sarah grumbled to herself as she had a pee, but he was a morning grouch and didn't like too many demands on his little grey brain cells before half past ten in the morning.

Flushing the loo, she wandered over to the cooker and placed a pot of cold water on the ring to boil. Bending down, she checked the mouse-trap in the cupboard under the sink.

"Damn those little rascals," she muttered.

Yet again, the bacon fat and hard cheese had been swiped from the front of the trap, yet no squashed mouse stared glassy-eyed at Sarah from beneath the spring-loaded bar. They were too cunning to be caught in the traps.

In the first week, Sarah had caught six mice. At first, she had asked Mrs Afandi's two eldest sons to come and check the traps, empty them if necessary and reset them for the next night, but after a couple of days, Sarah decided to learn a new skill of setting and emptying mouse-traps – distasteful and all as it was. And she learnt her skill well, because she caught four mice in the following few days. There had been a lull for a while then. Apart from those of the Afandi children, there were no sounds of marching feet to waken Sarah from her slumber. Her box of cereal and other sundries in her food cupboard remained intact and no telltale little black droppings appeared. Sarah was beginning to think that she had won the battle and rid her room of intruders, but her time of peace didn't last long.

The mice returned.

Or rather, a new family of mice arrived.

This new family was of a different breed, a different blood ran through their veins. These were mice to be reckoned with – supermice. They were crafty little beggars, tenacious and invincible. They marched around the flat at night with a confidence that made Sarah question her own right to be there. They scattered her cereal and bread and rice to the four corners of the cupboard and generously sprinkled their droppings in places Sarah didn't think it was possible for mice to sprinkle droppings.

But worst of all, these mice were capable of robbing the bacon fat and hard cheese from the traps without even setting them off. And that, Sarah found difficult to tolerate. She had even tried it herself one evening. She had donned rubber gloves for protection and tried, using Mal's Swiss army knife and a cocktail stick, to remove the food from the trap but she had failed. Three times she tried, and three times she had only succeeded in setting off the trap, once even catching the tip of the rubber glove in the bar as it snapped down with a force that was frightening. Sarah had yelped in fright, and then managed to tear a hole in the rubber glove as she attempted to extricate it.

Sarah couldn't understand how she – with a million more brain cells than a mere mouse – was unable to remove a piece of food from a machine invented by humans, while a dimwitted little piece of squeaking fluff, that was probably one of the lowest forms of life next to an amoeba, could outwit the trap. New strategies were called for, Sarah decided as she pulled on her jeans and brushed her hair. Perhaps she should start thinking of rat poison, she considered as she gulped down a couple of mouthfuls of coffee.

Or larger traps with serrated jaws.

Or a cat.

She looked at her watch as she ran downstairs and out the front door. Just half past eight. Luckily, she didn't have to get the tube or bus anywhere. She ran up to the main road, turned past the square where men and women were already assembling aluminium rods to make the stalls for the market later that morning, round by the clock tower and across at the lights to the corner where Bakhtiar's deli and sandwich bar was located.

"You are late," was Bakhtiar's first greeting as Sarah arrived in the door, panting.

"Only by two minutes," she retorted, checking her watch. "It's not yet a quarter to."

Bakhtiar paused and looked briefly at Sarah as he sliced a sausage sandwich in two. He shook his head gravely.

"You are cheeky also. Too cheeky for an employee."

Sarah grinned at him and went into the rear of the shop to don her apron and tie back her long hair. She enjoyed working for Bakhtiar. He was generally crabby, but had a smudge of humour in him too. They got on well.

When she returned, there were two regular customers in the shop. While she took orders for their lunches, Bakhtiar himself disappeared to the rear from where Sarah knew he wouldn't emerge until after ten. He always disappeared as soon as she arrived, going upstairs to his living quarters. He liked to lie down and read the daily paper while he listened to Wagnerian operas on his CD player. Sarah didn't mind. In fact, she preferred to be left on her own to wake up properly and to gather her thoughts for the day. She generally fixed herself a coffee and a sandwich for breakfast, but that was after the morning regulars had ordered their lunches.

The deli was very busy from the time she arrived until about half past nine by which time most people had started work. Sarah would spend that time writing up dockets, taking money for lunches and issuing receipts. The orders were pinned up on a cork notice-board on the wall and after half past nine, Sarah would start making them up – buttering bread and spreading or spooning on the various fillings, packing little cartons full of paté or mixed salad or coleslaw. Each order was placed in a brown paper bag with the customer's docket stapled to the top and put sitting on a large plastic tray that slid into the fridge. Bakhtiar joined Sarah at about half ten and while she made up lunches, he would check the accounts.

Money matters were not obviously Bakhtiar's strong point and he would curse and mutter angrily when the figures on the pages didn't match with the money in the till, which they rarely did. Inevitably, he would end up being short of a couple of twenties, or sometimes even more. Sometimes, he'd ask Sarah to check his adding up. When she did, she'd usually arrive at the same figure as he did, but the cash to hand was significantly less.

"Perhaps you're being robbed," she suggested helpfully on one occasion.

"Well, if I am, you're the one robbing me," he snarled back. "No one else has access to the till."

Sarah said no more about it after that, but she knew from Bakhtiar's noises that his accounts were frequently incorrect.

Lunch orders placed before half past nine were delivered to local offices between one and two by a scrawny youth on an ancient black butcher's bicycle. He balanced the plastic tray between the handlebars and the front of the wide basket and wobbled off to deliver.

At half past twelve, a mad rush started when it seemed as if every local worker who had failed to place an order that morning converged on the little deli, cramming it full so that often the queue spilled out the door and down the street. The rush continued unabated until half-past two, and during that entire time, Bakhtiar and Sarah would feverishly halve, butter, fill, slice, close and bag hundreds of sandwiches and baps and rolls. The one redeeming feature of the place was that there were no dining facilities on the premises, so there were no dishes to be cleared away or coffee-stained tabletops to wipe. Everything ordered was to take away so the turn-over was fast and efficient.

By two-thirty, the place looked as if it had been the scene of a civil war with heaps of butter-knives, serving spoons, empty dishes and bowls heaped in the sink, crumbs everywhere, and dollops of mayonnaise or drips of dressing or slivers of meat littering the worktops and the floor. The scrawny youth on the butcher's bike returned with the empty tray and Bakhtiar fixed them all salads and sandwiches and coffees. They shut up shop then and sat in the back room eating and looking at papers and listening to the radio.

Bakhtiar never introduced the scrawny youth to

Sarah, nor Sarah to the scrawny youth; he considered such introductions an unnecessary waste of his energy, so it was left to themselves whether they wished to know each other or not. He knew both of them and that was sufficient for him.

At first, Sarah was shy about talking to the youth and merely acknowledged him with a brief nod each day. He was black with a gold nose-ring, and insisted on bringing his butcher's bike right into the back room with them each day. Sarah thought this ridiculous. The front of the shop was locked up, so nobody could steal it, and it seemed pointless manouvring it round the counter area and through the narrow hallway into the one room they used. The room was cramped enough for the three of them without a great lumbering butcher's bike propped against the wall, but she didn't feel she should say anything as she didn't know him and Bakhtiar made no comment.

The delivery boy said nothing to Sarah either, failing even to acknowledge her daily nod. At first, she was a little peeved at this – he could at least have welcomed her to the job, but after a while, she realised that he said nothing to anybody – not even to Bakhtiar or to the customers. Every day, he would wordlessly arrive at one o'clock exactly and take the tray out of the fridge, unpin the delivery sheet from the cork notice-board and cycle off without a hello or a goodbye. He never checked if all of the orders had been made up and placed on the tray: if the order was on the tray at one o'clock, then fine, it was delivered, and if not, then tough, it was left in the shop. After being caught out twice by leaving two orders on the top of the fridge rather than on the tray inside the fridge and later finding them undelivered, Sarah always made sure that she had all the deliveries made up by ten to one in case he ever sneaked in and whisked the tray off while she was busy with someone else.

After a couple of weeks sharing lunch, newspapers and a bicycle with him in the cramped back room, Sarah decided it was time to get to know this tacit person a little better. Even to know his name would be a help, would give him some form of identity. It could also mean that she might get to know somebody in London apart from Bakhtiar, Mrs Afandi and her seven children. Sarah felt in need of company and was heartily sick of sitting in her little bed-sit in the evenings. It wasn't how she had imagined her new life in the city of London to be. She had envisaged herself partying late every night in the clubs and bars, wearing sassy little dresses and sipping exotic cocktails. Sitting alone in a grotty, mice-infested bed-sit with nothing to do but reset mouse-traps, write imaginary letters that were never sent and wash her clothes wasn't life as she wished to live it.

So the next afternoon, when he came in with his bike and sat down to eat after propping it against the wall, Sarah opened the conversation.

"Hi there," she started.

The scrawny youth ignored her and took a mighty bite out of his sandwich. Bakhtiar looked up briefly.

"Hi," he replied flatly before returning to his paper. Silence settled in the room once again, broken only by the munch of food and the turning of pages.

Sarah turned pink and took a mouthful of her own food. That's not what was supposed to happen, she thought, feeling stupid. She paused before making another attempt.

"I'm Sarah. What's your name?" she asked, leaning right over to try and gain eye contact with the delivery boy whose gaze was directed at the orange design on the carpet. He slowly lifted his eyes and regarded her thoughtfully, chewing silently as he did so. Sarah felt herself turning pink again, from embarrassment and from the peculiar position she had adopted where her head was lower than her knees. She straightened up and saw with a sense of relief that his brown eyes moved upwards also – she had half expected his gaze to remain staring at the place where her head had been but was pleased to notice that she had made some contact with him. His expression did not change and apart from his eyes, his only movements were the mastication of his jaws.

"Flea."

Sarah hadn't truly expected him to say anything, even though she was leaning forwards in anticipation. The single word surprised her.

Was this his name?

Or a greeting?

Or some form of opinion he was expressing?

Was he merely telling her to buzz off and mind her own business?

"What did you say?" she asked.

The boy's expression did not change. He merely repeated the word.

"Flea."

Sarah nodded as though she understood him. It wouldn't do to insult him now by failing to understand him after finally managing to communicate – however erratically. She smiled encouragingly.

"I see, I see," she continued, even though she didn't. She

paused, considering her next move. Any further comment from her had to be sufficiently open-ended to indicate that she knew something of where this conversation was leading, although she hadn't a clue. Certainly, the boy who regarded her as he chewed was of no help.

"Anything else?" she asked hopefully.

He swallowed his mouthful.

"What d'you want to know my other names for?" he demanded.

Sarah shook her head, protesting, understanding him suddenly.

"I don't, I don't. Flea is just fine. No need to know any other names. Great. Hi, Flea."

She let out a long breath. She was on familiar ground again. They were still on the topic of names. He had answered her question as asked. No frills or fancy stuff about him anyway, Sarah mused as she resumed eating. It was a start.

Once she knew Flea's name, he was more relaxed with her and frequently greeted her with a grunt in the mornings when he came in. After work in the evenings, he sometimes walked with her as far as the market square, before they made their respective ways home.

Sarah thought Flea had a great life. He was a real party animal who frequently stayed out at parties until five or six in the morning, catching the night bus home to grab a couple of hours' sleep before work. His low profile during the day was often due to serious hangover. Sarah began to recognise when he'd had a bad night of it from his washed-out appearance.

These parties appealed to Sarah. They sounded exciting and she plagued him to bring her to one.

"They're not for someone like you," he replied evasively.

They were on their way home at the time. Sarah halted her steps to challenge Flea's response.

"What do you mean 'someone like me'?" she asked. "What kind of a someone am I?"

Flea kicked against the kerb.

"Things go on at them – I don't know if you . . . "

He trailed off.

"Go on, say it. Spit it out. What are you talking about – what kind of things?"

Sarah was bugged by his comment.

"You're still kind of young, Sarah. And these parties . . . "

"I'm the same age as you, Flea."

Flea adjusted the light on the front of his bike as he prepared to cycle home. He shook his head.

"I don't mean in years. Yes, then I am the same age as you. But as a person, I think I'm older than you."

"What are you on about?" Sarah demanded angrily. She was furious. "After all, I'm living on my own, earning a living, working full-time . . . what more is there?"

But her words were lost to the wind. Flea had cycled off, vanishing into the darkening evening and leaving Sarah standing indignantly in the middle of the empty market square.

And so home she went to an empty bedsit, with a MacDonalds takeaway, to lie on her bed and listen to the Afandi children upstairs as they squabbled about what television channels to look at. She thought about her own family at home and wondered if they too were squabbling in front of the telly. She doubted it. Lee,

Alice and her mum were the real telly addicts in her house. They all watched programmes at different times, so there was little conflict. Lee loved the children's television on early in the afternoons when he got home from school and he took his afternoon snack of cheese and crackers in to the coffee table in front of the TV, where he had the remote control to himself and no one to disturb him.

Sarah's mum was mad into the American chat-shows broadcast on cable television. She thought Oprah Winfrey was brilliant and would leave the kitchen door wide open in the evenings as she prepared the dinner so that if anything exciting came on, she could race in to watch it, wiping her hands on her apron as she perched on the arm of the settee to watch.

Alice was the one who followed the regular soaps from Australia, such as *Home and Away* and *Neighbours*. She went mad if she missed an episode.

Sarah smiled to herself as she thought of them all. Maybe she'd write to them to say hello and let them know how she was doing. She frowned. No, writing would not be a good idea. A letter would have the postmark stamped on it and they might know where she was then. Phoning was safer, within Sarah's control. She could choose when to hang up, when to cut them off if the going got a bit tough. She could pick a good time to ring, when she knew they were all in, when she wouldn't be interrupted. Yes, phoning was best. Maybe she'd give them a ring soon. Maybe she'd tell them all about her new job and the flat, about Flea and Bakhtiar.

The next morning at the deli, Flea came in as usual

to collect his tray of deliveries. Sarah ignored him, smarting still from his comment the previous evening, and continued chopping peppers.

"Hello, Sarah," he said.

Sarah ignored him. Who did he think he was anyway – swanning in all cheerful and friendly when only the previous night he had told her that parties weren't for someone like her?

Flea didn't appear to notice the rebuff and went on.

"I'm going to a house-party on Friday next. It's in the Sheds. Do you want to come along?"

Sarah stopped chopping and looked at him suspiciously.

"Is this party more suitable for someone like me than your usual ones?" she enquired.

Flea turned to the fridge and began sliding out the tray.

"You can make up your own mind about that."

The rain drummed down on the hood of his anorak as Lee walked up the road to his house. His shoes squelched and he deliberately splashed through the puddles on the roadside. The water seeped through his socks at his ankles above where his shoes ended, but Lee didn't care.

It had rained all day and, when school ended, Lee had waited at the gates of the schoolyard in case his mother collected him. Since Sarah had left, his mother didn't like him going to Seán's house after school because Seán's mother always asked if they'd heard from Sarah. Lee always had to tell her that no, they'd not heard anything. Anyway, Mrs Bailey had only worked part-time since then and was usually free to collect Lee from school if the weather was really bad.

Today, the weather *was* really bad with cold grey rain that fell in drenching sheets, but she didn't collect him. He had waited and waited at the school gates until all the other parents' cars had gone. Seán's mother offered to drop him home, but Lee refused, afraid that he might miss his own mother if she did turn up.

But she didn't, and after standing on his own for over half an hour, Lee decided to walk home.

As he trudged up his road, he peered through the rain at his house. The rain trickled down his fringe and dripped into his eyes, blurring his vision and making him look down again. He stepped off the path and walked along by the gutter, watching the rainwater as it sluiced over the toes of his shoes and washed against his grey uniform socks. Lee stopped and turned sideways, letting his feet form a dam against which the water gathered and deepened until it overflowed his shoes and cascaded onwards. He winced at the sudden coldness of the soaking water creeping over his ankles. Stepping on to the grass verge, he shook most of the rainwater from his shoes and crossed the footpath. Turning in at his own gate, he opened the front door with the latchkey that hung on a ribbon pinned inside his pocket.

Lee could hear voices coming from the sitting-room and so he walked in to see who was there. His mother was perched on the edge of the armchair beside the empty grate, talking to two people who sat on the settee with their backs to the door. A tray with tea and a plate of biscuits rested on the small table between them.

"Hello, darling," his mother began, looking towards him immediately and holding out her arms. Lee looked at her as he walked over. Her eyes were red-rimmed and she looked upset.

"Are you OK?" Lee questioned, looking indignantly towards the two strangers who had obviously upset his mother.

"Yes, I'm fine," she assured him, but she didn't look fine. And she didn't sound fine either. Her voice was watery and weak. Lee frowned at the strangers. One of them smiled and introduced herself as Mary. The other one said nothing. She was holding a clipboard and nodded wordlessly to Lee.

His mother spoke again, feeling his wet coat. "Lee, you're soaked. Why don't you slip out to the kitchen and hang up your coat to dry, dear? Then pop upstairs and change. I'll be finished shortly."

Lee was always suspicious when his mother told him to "slip" or "pop" anywhere. It usually only happened when she was a bit on edge or trying to be nice but was really feeling awful. Otherwise she told him to "go" or "get" or "run" instead. Without another word, he "slipped" out and "popped" into the kitchen.

The breakfast dishes were heaped in the sink, unwashed. He felt the radiator, but it was cold, so he took off his soaking coat and hung it over the back of one of the chairs. He looked at it for a moment, and then spread a sheet of yesterday's newspaper on the floor beneath it to catch the drips. Dumping his schoolbag beside the fridge and kicking off his sodden shoes, he went upstairs, but he was only halfway up when the phone rang.

Charging downstairs, Lee picked up the receiver.

"Hello?"

"Hi, Lee. Are you home from school long?"

"Hi, dad. No, only just in."

"And how's your mum?"

Lee was feeling cold and he was grumpy about having had to walk home from school in the driving rain. Now all his father wanted to know was how his mother was – he didn't even ask how Lee was.

Or how he got on in school that day.

Or if he got home safely.

"Mum's busy talking to some people. She didn't collect me. I waited and waited, but she didn't turn up. I

66

walked home on my own and my feet are all wet. She just told me to go into the kitchen and wait. Now I'll probably get pneumonia and die."

His dad wasn't very sympathetic, which made Lee grumpier.

"Come on now, you're a big lad. You're well able to walk home from school on your own. Pop upstairs and have a hot bath and you'll be right as rain in no time. Ask your mum to slip out to the phone for a moment, will you?"

Pop. Slip. They were all at it. Something was definitely wrong.

Lee stuck his head in the sitting-room door.

"Dad's on the phone," he announced loudly without waiting to see if they were talking. "He wants a word with you."

As his mother made her way out to the phone, Lee scuttled upstairs. He knew he had been rude in front of strangers and he didn't want to hang around to be given out to. He went into the bathroom and turned on the hot tap to run his bath. He got a clean towel from the airing cupboard and brought his bathrobe into the bathroom. As he was crossing the landing, he could hear his mother's voice as she spoke on the phone.

" . . . social workers to check if things were OK here before Sarah left . . . all sorts of questions, all afternoon . . . "

Lee paused and leaned over the banisters, listening. His father was talking at that moment because his mother was silent. She spoke again.

" . . . it's been awful. Questions and questions . . . " she broke off then and it sounded as if she was crying. Lee felt sneaky about listening, so he went into the bathroom and locked the door. He felt shivery when he thought of his mum, all upset because of those two strangers, and his skin went goose-pimply as he peeled off his damp uniform.

By the time he had finished his bath and was dressed in a cosy track suit, his mother was back in the sitting-room. She called as he passed on his way to the kitchen.

"Lee."

Lee hesitated. He didn't really fancy going into the room again. He might not escape being given out to for being rude and it would be so embarrassing in front of strangers.

"Lee?"

There was no escape. Lee groaned and went into the sitting-room again, keeping his head down. The strangers were still there and they sat silently as his mother spoke.

"Dad is coming home early today," she told him. "Try and tidy up the kitchen for me before he gets here. You're a great boy."

Lee couldn't believe his luck. He'd got away with it and his mother had even told him he was great. There was no accounting for it. By the time his father arrived home, Lee had packed the dishwasher and was sitting at the kitchen table doing his homework.

"Why are you wearing Clem's anorak?" was the first question his father asked him.

"Because mine is wet," Lee replied, chewing at the top of his pencil as he answered.

"You'll get lead poisoning," his father told him.

"From Clem's anorak?" Lee was surprised about that. He'd thought Clem's anorak was the same type as his.

"From chewing pencil tops," his father explained, pointing to the splinters of wood that Lee had spat out on his copybook. "Why are you wearing an anorak at all?"

"Because the house is freezing and I don't know how to turn on the central heating," Lee told him, gathering up the splinters of wood into a little heap. He rubbed his nose, which was still cold, and then shaped his heap of chewed pencil wood into a funeral pyre.

"Why didn't you light the gas fire instead?"

Lee looked at his father indignantly. "I'm not allowed to touch it, remember? You told me never to touch the gas fire or I'd set the house on fire. And mum is too busy to disturb."

"OK, OK, point taken," his father responded. "I'll light it for you now."

At the same time, his mother emerged from the sitting-room. When she saw her husband, her eyes filled up and she gave him a big hug.

"Yeuch!" Lee said, returning rapidly to his sums. "I hate all this mucky-love stuff."

His parents disappeared into the dining-room to have a quick chat before his mother returned to the sitting-room again. His father came quickly into the kitchen and lit the gas fire for Lee, then explained.

"Lee, I'm going to meet our visitors for a while. They want to talk a bit about Sarah. Are you all right here on your own?"

"'Course I am. What time is Clem coming home?"

His father was already halfway into the sitting-room. He called back a reply.

"I don't know – whenever he feels like it."

As it happened, it was well after Lee's bedtime when Clem left college that evening. He had stayed on in the library taking some notes, and then he'd had a couple of pints in the students' bar before leaving for home.

The rain had stopped at last and Clem cycled through the wet streets, his wheels swishing on the tarmac. It was after eleven and the roads were quiet. Street lights were reflected in the puddles and the air was washed and clean.

For the umpteenth time that day, Clem thought about Sarah – wondered where she was and what she was doing. He didn't know where she might have gone, nor even why. Sometimes she had these crazy notions about leading a different kind of life, and although Clem knew her ideas were important to her, he didn't really understand why.

Her leaving home as suddenly as she did had thrown the whole family into disarray. Her parents had phoned the police immediately after her disappearance to help them find out if Sarah was safe, or if something terrible had happened to her. There were then a few nightmare days when the police had turned to questioning the whole family and checking out how Sarah'd got on with everybody.

Clem had got really annoyed.

"They're meant to be here to help us find Sarah, for God's sake, not to interrogate us. We reported her missing – it's hardly as if we've bumped her off and buried her body in the garden," he complained.

"I suppose they have to check every possibility," Alice replied with remarkable insight. "Maybe we're covering up some dastardly deed – they have to be sure."

"I bet we really look like a family capable of murder and mayhem," Clem answered sarcastically, "considering our extensive criminal records."

As it happened, the police wanted to ascertain if Sarah had confided in any of the family about her intentions, if she had mentioned her unhappiness. The sergeant in charge of the case had interviewed each of them in turn about Sarah's last known movements and enquired if she'd had a fight with any of them, or if she'd just broken up with a boyfriend, or had been expelled from school. In fact, if they could recall anything in recent times that may have upset or traumatised her sufficiently to make her want to leave home so abruptly. Then he'd checked and crosschecked their individual stories and come back to double-check anyone whose story didn't match with the others.

They were all nervous wrecks in case they forgot any minor detail that might indicate they were lying or trying to cover up something. Clem was the most informative, as he was the closest to Sarah, but even he could give little in the way of concrete help.

The police extended their interviews to include her teachers and school-friends, as well as local friends and extended family. That was when Mr Bailey got a little edgy and was convinced their questioning was far beyond the norm. He began to worry that his family appeared dysfunctional and that it looked as if he and his wife were inadequate parents.

"No indeed, sir," the superintendent had assured him. "These are just routine questions that we put to anyone in a situation like yours. We have to satisfy ourselves that Sarah's not been unhappy or isolated at home, that she'd no major reason to run away."

The first breakthrough came when the police interviewed Karen. They were systematically making their way around all of Sarah's classmates and talking to each of them in turn. Karen's turn came on the second day of interviews and she nervously knocked on the door of the office that they were using in the school.

"Come in," called the policewoman sitting inside.

Karen entered and sat down, smiling hesitantly. She suspected instantly that the police knew she was the one they were after. She felt as if "guilty" was branded across her forehead. Her hands felt all sweaty and her heart was thumping, but still she said nothing.

"Hello there," said the policewoman. "And what's your name?"

"Karen . . . Karen Vaughan."

"Fine. Sit down please, Karen."

The policewoman checked her list of names and ticked Karen's off.

"I see here that you're a good friend of Sarah's," she began, glancing up at Karen.

"Mmm," Karen responded carefully. She didn't trust herself to speak.

"So, do you have any idea what happened to your friend, then?"

Karen couldn't put up with the tension. They were bound to find out the truth sooner or later. Or to insist that she take a lie detector test which she would undoubtedly fail. There was no point in covering up.

"Yes, I do," Karen blurted out immediately, surprising

even herself with her willingness to reveal all. "I helped her to run away." Well, she decided, espionage as a career is obviously out of the window for me.

It all came out in the wash then. Karen felt very guilty and upset when she realised that, by helping her friend, she had actually put her in possible danger. Christy was duly contacted, having returned that morning from his trip to Britain. He was genuinely surprised at all he learned and claimed that he never knew Sarah was running away from home unknown to her parents.

"Anyway," he retorted, "isn't she over sixteen? Surely she's entitled to leave home at that age if she wants to."

"She's still legally a child, sir, and as such, her parents have full responsibility for her care and protection," said the superintendent. "Your encouragement has not made their job any easier. It's important that we establish that Sarah has left of her own accord and not because of any undue duress or neglect."

"She wanted to leave all right," Christy assured them. "Couldn't wait to get going on her new life – and good luck to her. Nice young one. I hope she knows how to take care of herself, though."

"That's our concern exactly, sir."

All Christy could tell them was that he'd brought Sarah as far as Birmingham, from where she planned to catch a train to London. After that, he had no idea of her movements.

As Clem locked his bike in the shed in the back garden that night, he looked up at the house. The downstairs lights were out, which meant that everyone had gone to bed.

He opened the back door, locking it behind him, and, without bothering to turn on the kitchen light, left his jacket on the table. He was just about to make his way upstairs when a soft noise in the sitting-room halted him.

The door to the room was closed. No light shone underneath it. Clem froze and listened again, straining his ears to try to identify what it was.

There. He heard it again. A sort of clinking noise. There was somebody in there.

Clem's heart began to pound. His hand, poised on the newel post, was immediately sweaty. Was it a burglar? The hall clock behind him suddenly chimed a quarter past midnight, causing Clem to leap in fright, his hair roots even responding to the start, his ears aching from the unexpected loudness.

Taking a deep breath, Clem stepped silently across the carpet and lightly rested his hand on the door handle. Softly, he pressed it downwards and, in the one movement, opened it and stepped into the room.

The curtains were drawn back, revealing the street outside. The room was in deep shadow, lit dimly by the orange glow from the streetlight. Clem's eyes flitted around the room, taking in the VCR, the stereo, the shut window. Nothing had been stolen, no obvious signs of forced entry.

His eyes rested on a figure sitting still in the armchair. The figure didn't move, not having heard Clem's stealthy entrance. The person in the chair leaned forwards, head down and resting on hands, elbows on knees. A half-filled whiskey glass glinted on the table beside the armchair, the ice floating in it clinking gently against the side.

It was Clem's father.

"Dad . . . are you OK?"

Mr Bailey started, jerking his head up and looking in bewilderment at Clem, who still stood in the doorway.

"Son, you're late home," Mr Bailey said.

"What are you doing up? I thought everyone would be in bed hours ago," Clem asked, pulling up a seat and sitting next to his father in the dim light.

"We've had a tough evening of it," his father responded. "Thought I'd have a drink on my own to relax before heading upstairs."

"Any word about Sarah?" Clem asked, knowing full well that's what his father meant when he said he'd had a tough evening.

"Ach," his father said. "Bloody social workers round here all afternoon quizzing your mother and me about family life and Sarah and how we treated her. Seems some teacher in the school had concerns about Sarah because she appeared – what was the word they used? – repressed or depressed or suppressed or something. That and her running away has them all up in arms and they're checking that we haven't been too hard on her."

Clem took a deep breath and threw his eyes up to heaven.

"For crying out loud," he cried. "Have they not more to be doing with their time than checking on you?"

Mr Bailey smiled wearily.

"They're only doing their job, Clem. Upset your

mother quite a bit, let me tell you, but we'd be madder with them if there was a real case of abuse and they failed to check on it."

He drained the last of the whiskey from his glass and stood up.

"Anyway, let's make our way to bed, shall we? We both have work in the morning."

Sarah sat lopsidedly in a corner off the main dancing area and looked dizzily around her. The music was thumping wildly overhead, blaring out of the speakers. The floor vibrated with the noise and the stamping of feet.

It was great.

She didn't understand what Flea had been talking about when he suggested that this wasn't right for her. Since arriving, she'd been having a brilliant night. Everyone there was great, really friendly and having a good time. The music was great. The drink was great. The atmosphere was great. The people especially were really great. They danced non-stop for ages and ages – far longer than Sarah could keep going without a breather.

From her place on the floor, she watched the dancers as they moved crazily in strangely obscene rhythms, gyrating with each other and twisting their limbs together and apart. Others leaped into the air, absorbed in their own movements. They jerked their arms and heads around, their eyes closed, jumping up and down, knocking against smooching couples and reeling around.

Sarah grinned, enjoying the sensation of the bass notes thudding insistently in her ears and her chest. The rhythm was slightly faster than her own pulse and it gave her a real buzz. The half-empty plastic beaker slid slowly out of her hand and toppled over, spilling vodka and orange in a pool next to her on the grimy floor. Sarah hazily watched it puddle and trickle against her leg where it seeped through her jeans and felt warm.

She grinned.

Maybe she should get up and try to find Flea, she considered sluggishly. It was almost half an hour since he had left her with her drink while he went to have a pee.

Turning her head, she looked to her left, peering through the masses of writhing bodies in a vain attempt to see him, not even knowing the direction he had gone. There was an open doorway leading to another huge dance area. A couple stood in the doorway, wrapped together. Sarah couldn't see their faces, both because they were so close together and because it was too dim to see properly in the flashing lights. Their hands explored each other urgently. The girl was fat with shaved stubbly hair and she had her back against the door-frame. There was some kind of tattoo etched blackly on to her scalp. The guy stood against her, his head buried in her neck. In slow motion, the girl lifted her leg slowly and wrapped it around the guy's waist.

Sarah shifted her gaze beyond the couple and into the far room.

That was when she saw Flea.

He was standing sideways to her, his head bent, talking to two people Sarah hadn't seen before. One of them had a packet in his hands. They were discussing something. It looked as though they were having some kind of an argument. Flea was shaking his head and saying something. The other guys responded by shrugging their shoulders and indicating the little package they held. Flea said something back, his face angry, his words lost in the cacophony of music and voices and thumps that filled the place but said with great energy as if he was shouting loudly.

Sarah was curious, interested in what was going on. She leaned forward to better see around the entwined couple in the doorway.

Maybe she should try and help out, she decided. Help Flea – seeing as he had been so nice as to bring her along the party. Perhaps she could sort out their little argument.

Sarah awkwardly stumbled to her feet, her head swirling with the drink and the music, the flashing lights and the heat. She turned towards Flea again. Now, there was only one guy with him. The other one had vanished. The guy who remained was very thin. Whenever Flea talked to him, his sharp eyes scanned the crowds around them, checking who might be watching. For an instant his gaze caught Sarah's eye. She froze with the intensity of the look, with the unexpected blueness that glittered and was hard like tiny chips of blue glass. But she held no interest for him and he shifted his focus, moving his gaze on to linger a moment on another face in the crowd. At that moment, Sarah thought better of trying to sort out any argument. That guy with the diamond-hard eyes didn't look too friendly and her sudden appearance might only complicate matters. She'd find a loo instead, she decided, and perhaps by then they would have tired of their squabbling. She steadied herself against the wall. It was wet with condensation. Sarah pushed off, wiping her hand on the backside of her jeans, and moved in a purposeful manner towards the entrance where they had come in.

Once, she glanced back at Flea and his friend but they had gone, soaked up by the blue haze of steam and cigarette smoke and the masses of dancing, writhing, twisting, smooching, sweating bodies.

There was a crowd of girls sitting in a circle against the wall inside the main door. Sarah bent down, wobbling a bit, and yelled at one of them to tell her where the toilets were. The girl she asked had a safety pin through her right nostril which was attached by a fine silver chain to another safety pin stuck through the top of her right ear. Sarah was so close to her that she could see the tiny hole in the girl's nose where the safety pin went in. She was fascinated and stared at it while she was talking. It looked horrible, all red and inflamed, and the chain dragged out of it, stretching the tiny hole downwards. The girl looked at Sarah for a moment through heavily-mascared lashes, carefully considering her question, before turning back to the others. She repeated Sarah's question to them and they all shrieked, laughing hysterically.

"Show her where it is," one of them giggled at the others.

Two of them stood up, grabbing each other to steady themselves and moved off, pulling Sarah along with them. One of them was the girl with the safety pins.

"Come on," they urged her.

They left the building and walked along one side of it. After the heat of inside, the night air was freezing and Sarah shivered, stumbling after the two girls. They walked the entire length of the building, through long grass and gravel, turning right at the end to where a huge brick archway formed a wide, high tunnel – open at each end – linking their building with the next. In the tunnel, three oil drums were on fire, crackling and spitting sparks and flames. There were people gathered around the oil drums, some of them sitting on planks of wood or tyres or old gas cylinders, others standing up. The tunnel area stank of burning rubber and urine.

Sarah's two guides bypassed the knots of people around the fires and moved to the other end of the tunnel. She followed them wordlessly, stumbling slightly. There, they pointed out a heap of junk and debris, old prams and sheets of corrugated iron, cans and tyres. Thistles and nettles grew in profusion amongst the garbage.

"There's your toilet," one of them shouted, laughing.

"It's communal so make sure you squat upwind of the lads – their aim isn't so good," the other one giggled.

They clutched each other with mirth and stumbled back through the tunnel, leaving Sarah at the junk-heap.

"There's plenty of nettles for toilet paper," they shouted at her as they vanished from sight round the corner of the building.

Sarah stood for a moment, not sure of what to do. She wished she knew where Flea had got to, but felt she had to let some time pass between the funny business she had noticed and going to look for him.

She knew that she would have to find him because he knew where they were and for that reason, he, presumably, knew how to get home.

Sarah didn't.

She didn't even know where she was.

To get to the Sheds, they had travelled by night bus for miles and miles, and then walked for ages alongside a black, oily river. The area was like some enormous industrial wasteland, half-derelict. Ghost buildings leaned towards them and vast structures of steel like giant skeletons of starved and emaciated buildings groaned eerily in the wind. They had travelled that far alone, but as they neared the Sheds, they met up with more and more people, all heading in the same direction. They crossed an old iron bridge on to cobblestones, passing huge warehouses and dark depots. The only light had been occasional security lights fixed high up on the warehouses. These switched on as they passed, suffusing the area in a blinding brightness that made it far harder to see when they were plunged into darkness again.

Unexpectedly, they had come upon the Sheds.

They had turned a dark, silent corner and the music had blasted them in the face, thudding and hammering. Light and heat spilled out from one of the warehouses, the huge industrial doors flung open. There were hordes of young people moving and dancing and talking and sitting and shouting, milling about and thronging into the building.

Sarah followed Flea as he plunged into the masses. He knew a lot of people. He took some money from her and got them both plastic cups of drink – Sarah didn't know from where because she couldn't see any bar. For a while, they stood around. Flea nodded and grunted to several people who came over and gave him friendly thumps. He didn't introduce Sarah to anyone, and nobody passed any remark about her being with Flea.

Sarah was a bit on edge at first, uncomfortable in this madhouse of noise and drink and strange people. She stood wordlessly next to Flea, not letting him out of immediate reach, looking warily around her.

After about half an hour, when no one had stabbed her, mugged her, grabbed her purse or tried to rape her, she relaxed and began to enjoy herself. She moved among the crowds of people who were leaping and moving and jumping around the floor. Sarah enjoyed that. It was crazy and zany and fun. Everybody was sweaty, with their hair plastered against their heads, and the music made you want to move wildly. Flea got them more drinks and after a while, Sarah felt herself floating a little bit. When she closed her eyes, the glaring lights penetrated her lids and flashed and dazzled in mottled shades of red and yellow so that when she twirled her head, they rotated and spun around madly making her feel dizzy and slightly sick. When she opened her eyes, the whole place appeared to her as if seen through a film of gauze. People moved in time with the music – which was fast – but it also appeared to Sarah that they moved in slow motion, which didn't make sense. So she sat on the concrete floor against the wall while Flea said he'd be back in a few moments. Everyone else kept jumping around madly.

Now, here she stood in front of a junk-heap on her own at the end of a smelly tunnel, in the freezing cold, not sure what to do. She regretted not having organised the way back to her flat. It was so unlike her not to have planned her way home – usually she had decided in advance whether to get a bus or a taxi, in what direction and how much it was likely to cost. She usually knew the location of the place she was trying to leave. If Flea was involved in some dubious dealings or – worse still – if he had gone on home without her, what in the world would she do?

She hiccuped and swayed slightly, wondering what to do.

There was a noise from just outside the tunnel and Sarah swirled around, half-expecting someone to have crept up behind her. Her vision swam for a moment and it was a couple of seconds before she could focus again. But there was nobody there, just a wide dark expanse of windswept grass stretching into the night, shivering and shuddering from the rough stroking of the bitter wind. Sarah stepped to the mouth of the tunnel and looked up towards the sky. Clouds of inky black heaved past overhead, the edges of their high-piled shapes water-painted a ghostly white by the moon hidden behind them. Glimpses of dazzling white crescent sometimes gleamed out suddenly where the clouds were torn, but they were mainly heavy and deep, blotting out the cold light.

Again, Sarah heard a noise.

She listened, straining her eyes to see across the rippling grasses, straining her ears to hear the faint sound.

Was somebody moving around?

Or was it a shout?

Sarah stepped out of the mouth of the tunnel.

It came again from her right.

She turned.

There, in the darkness, huddled against the rough brickwork of the tunnel wall, two figures were standing.

Sarah paused just long enough to taste the flavour of their bitter mood, to smell the powerful odour of their anger. They spoke in raised, threatening voices, their words carrying towards her, half-snatched by the wind, half-reaching Sarah's ears. They gestured to each other with aggressive, violent movements.

Sarah shrank back against the wall, watching still but melting silently into the shadows. She knew both figures. She recognised the dark, curly hair of Flea and the thin, sharp features of the boy he had been arguing with inside. She knew she shouldn't be there, knew she had intruded and that she should move off silently, should withdraw; but still she stayed, watching, observing.

The argument continued unabated and appeared to centre on the same small package, held now by Flea. Abruptly, the stranger took one step back from Flea. There was a pause, a moment when the scene took on the appearance of a freeze-frame in a video.

Flea stood without moving.

The blue-eyed stranger looked like a hideous praying mantis, poised as he was in front of Flea, lit from behind in a sudden glare of cold white moonlight.

Sarah held her breath, but gasped involuntarily when she saw the sudden flash of metal, the glint of a stray moonbeam on the polished blade of a knife. It was held in the stranger's hand, not poised over his head as she had seen in films, but low down, dangerous and deadly, ready to be used. Without a single pause for thought, without a single consideration of his actions, without a single reflection on his movements, the thin stranger thrust the knife forward, moving it in a lethal curve towards the crouching Flea. The ice-white light of the moon caught the blade as it sliced through the air. A flashing arc of brightness traced the blade's path as it travelled ruthlessly into Flea, who moaned softly and sank down on his hunkers.

Sarah moaned too, an unexpected and primitive cry of shock and pain and disbelief. She clutched her stomach with one hand, her other hand held across her mouth, and watched with pure horror as the thin stranger withdrew the knife, its polished surface now dull and smeared. Coolly, he leaned across and wrenched from Flea's motionless hands the small package that had been the centre of the row.

It was then that Sarah retched, a dry, uncontrollable strangling sound that caught in her throat and gagged her.

She knew she was going to throw up.

She also knew she had been heard.

The stranger did not react instantly and, in a way, his slow reaction was even more frightening. When Sarah made the sound that betrayed her presence, he paused for an instant in his movements.

Paused just for a split second.

Hardly a break at all – merely a barely discernible delay in his actions, a minute slowing of his muscles.

Then he straightened up, jerking his jacket back on his sharp shoulders, and turned slowly, so, so slowly and deliberately towards Sarah, who stood motionless and petrified.

For the second time that evening, their eyes met just for an instant and again, Sarah felt a chill shiver down her spine as the ice-blue eyes fixed on hers. But this time, his gaze lingered on her, taking in her features, looking at her so that he would recognise her again.

And Sarah knew she would have to get out of there – fast.

Turning, she stumbled blindly back into the tunnel. Her hands groped the stinking, festering walls. Her feet stumbled and tripped over heaps of junk and debris. Ahead of her, she could see small groups of people standing around the burning oil drums. She could hear their voices echoing in the space created by the archway. She listened to her own harsh breathing, made louder beneath the high roof of the tunnel. Her footsteps sounded slow and clumsy. She wasn't able to move fast enough. She lifted her feet high, trying to step over the garbage that she couldn't see. The pounding of her feet and the jarring of her body made the vomit rise in her throat. It threatened to choke her and she frantically tried to control it. She couldn't stop, had to keep going. She gasped and swallowed hard. Behind her, she could hear the sounds of her pursuer, crashing through the undergrowth and rubbish. He was gaining on her with every stride so that she could now hear his own laboured breathing over her right shoulder. Sarah sobbed with terror. What would he do to her if he caught her? Stab her? Murder her, like he had Flea?

He wouldn't catch her. He couldn't catch her. Sarah wouldn't let him. She would escape. She would run and free herself from this waking nightmare. But where could she run to? She knew no one in this awful place. There was only Flea and now he lay slumped against the wall. Sarah realised that she had nowhere to go, no one to run to. She didn't know anyone else at this party. She didn't know how to get home. She didn't even know where she was, goddammit.

Behind her, there was a loud curse and a sudden crash as her pursuer tripped up and fell heavily on the ground. Sarah could hear him shouting and flinging pieces of earth and beer cans at her as he thrashed around, seeking to get up again as quickly as possible. A viciously-flung broken brick landed just ahead of her.

She dared herself to look back, steadying herself against the wall as she did so, but the darkness was too deep, beyond the reach of the flames, too complete at ground level so that she could only see a vague silhouette of someone moving around several yards from where she stood. Sarah turned, eager to use his fall to her advantage and widen the gap between them, but she too abruptly lost her balance and crashed down on to her knees. She winced in pain as the stone she landed on crunched against her kneecap. Everywhere was pitch black and Sarah could see nothing. The high weeds and coarse undergrowth blocked the flickering flames from the oil barrels. Sobbing now, desperate to escape, Sarah reached out blindly with one hand to find the wall, but her hand thrashed through the air, failing to make contact. She scrambled forwards on her knees, an ache shooting up one leg, and reached out with both hands to grasp the rough wall. Her sense of direction was confused in the darkness and she was unsure what way she was crawling. Maybe the wall was behind her. Maybe she had twisted round when she fell. Maybe she was crawling towards her enemy . . .

Sarah was frantic, hearing footsteps, knowing that her hunter was up and after her again. She was vulnerable on the ground with no hope of escape. She felt around wildly in the darkness and was surprised when her left hand made immediate contact with the wall just next to her. Groping her way upwards, Sarah went to stand up, but succeeded only in cracking her head painfully against brickwork immediately above her head. She fell again, dazed now, confused and felt around with her hands. She could feel rough walls on either side of her. About three feet above her head, she felt slimy, wet blocks – the ones she had cracked her head on. It seemed as though she was in some kind of deep alcove built into the side of the tunnel. In the darkness and confusion when she fell, Sarah had inadvertently crawled into it. She crouched there now, squatting on the damp earth, not believing her luck to have accidently found what was possibly the only bolthole in the entire place.

She shivered.

Her heart thumped madly against her ribcage, threatening to break it open, while her eyes stared wildly out towards the opening of the alcove to where the stranger stalked. She could hear his running steps, pausing now, then moving on a little, then stopping and moving back again to near where he had fallen. He was looking for her, was seeking her out. Sarah's breath was ragged and harsh, every breath hurting her as she tried to breathe quietly – nothing must betray her presence. Sweat soaked her back and arms and chest, rapidly chilling as she sat in the stillness of the damp alcove. Tears of sheer terror coursed down her cheeks.

She was too frightened to move, yet when she peeked out she discovered that she wasn't far from the fires in the oil-drums. She was near where groups of kids were standing and sitting and smoking and drinking and laughing and chatting. She could even hear snatches of their conversation, carried across to her on the breeze, the notes of their laughter, the snaps as they cracked open beer cans. But her heart skipped a beat when she suddenly saw a dark, slender figure approach the group and stand silently, lethally amongst them.

Sarah watched him, her teeth chattering. She could see his ribs heave from the run, could see his hands clench and unclench at his sides. His eyes were diamond-hard, the blueness of them intense. They travelled round the faces of everyone who stood at the fire, seeking her out, trying to find out if she had concealed herself among the anonymous people.

And in her little sanctuary, Sarah trembled, wishing she could move closer to the fires, wishing she could feel the burning heat on her face. Her legs felt weak, her knee throbbed, her stomach was sick. Still her heart pounded while her mind was whirling, her thoughts racing at a million miles an hour. What would happen now? Where could she go? There was nothing she could do. And what of Flea, lying in the cold and dark at the end of the building? Was he alive or . . . Sarah sobbed in the darkness. There was nothing she could do but wait.

Wait and see what happened.

Clem sat up in bed. He was suddenly awake, sleep whisked away from him like a sheet of gauze snatched by an invisible hand. It was the deepest part of the night. The red flashing light on his clock radio registered 3.45 am. He was alert and listening, every nerve pulsing, his heart racing, his breath coming in great gulps that frightened him.

What had woken him?

Straining his ears, he listened to pick up the slightest sound in the silent house. Had there been a noise outside? Perhaps one of the family was downstairs, having a drink of water?

But no sound reached his zinging ears.

He sat silently in the darkness until his breathing moved into a steadier rhythm. His heartbeat slowed down. His ears stopped twitching. Quietly, Clem pushed down the duvet and got out of bed. Walking over to the window, he pulled back the heavy curtains and leaned his forehead against the cold glass. Immediately the pane was frosted with his moist breath, a white circular smudge that grew as he breathed out, gradually misting his view of the dark road and the parked cars outside.

As usual his thoughts were immediately focused on Sarah. She was like some ubiquitous spirit, always her face pressing into his thoughts, always her image drifting in front of his eyes, both during idle and busy times; distracting him, upsetting him, unnerving him. Clem felt more distant and yet, at the same time, closer than he had ever felt to her before. He thought of her incessantly, dreamed of her nightly, smelt her presence in an empty room, caught a glimpse of her shadow in a shaft of sunlight. She was haunting him with an insistence that no longer comforted him.

When she first left, Clem's thoughts of Sarah were reassuring, reminding him of the times they had shared, the activities in which they had a common interest. In the beginning, he never failed to believe that she would return after a few weeks, after she had had her fingers burnt and decided she was too young to leave home and strike out on her own. He truly expected to arrive home from lectures one evening and find her sitting at the kitchen table, grinning sheepishly at him. And he looked forward to the times later on when they would laugh about her foolishness and he would tease her about her silly ideas.

But at the time he wasn't even aware of this belief of his, this unconscious refusal to believe that she had really gone. The memory of her laughing face, his mild annoyance at her recklessness, her strangely serious ideas about individuality, his on-going attempts to understand why she had left home without discussion or argument, agreement or plan, and his final utter failure to reach some level of understanding despite endless hours spent mulling and musing had been sufficient to buoy him through the early weeks of Sarah's leaving.

But as time dragged on with no news, no correspondence, no letter, no phone call, the hope he had nurtured gradually dwindled and he was left with the ghostly presence of his sister always in his thoughts that made it difficult to keep the same commitment to his studies.

Now, as he looked from his window down at the neat well-maintained front gardens, the dark shadows cast by the hedges on their trimmed lawns, Clem knew with certainty that something had happened to Sarah that night. Call it intuition, call it a primitive instinct long since obliterated by generations of civilisation and refinement, but Clem had a gut feeling, an awareness that there was something amiss, that something very bad had happened to Sarah. Although she had a great desire to turn her back on her family – the customs, the expectations, the mannerisms of her own clan – Sarah would never rid herself totally of what she herself was. It was ingrained in her – partly in her genes and partly in her environment and her upbringing. And because Clem was part of that upbringing, was of the same bloodline, he too shared a great deal of what she was about. There couldn't fail to be a link, a bond, some ethereal connection between them.

And it was that intangible tie which woke Clem up with the abruptness of a bucket of cold water. There was nobody downstairs. There was no noise outside on the street. He wasn't in the throes of a major coronary.

Sarah was in trouble.

One by one, the people gathered around the oil-drums began to drift inside. Sometimes others came out of the steaming, throbbing building to get some fresh air and stand for a while but, over a period of time, the numbers reduced. Eventually, there were only a dozen or so standing around. The fires had died down. Instead of high, leaping flames, there were glowing embers with the occasional flicker of green flame or shower of shooting sparks.

And still Sarah squatted in her den. Hidden. Safe.

And still the slender stranger stood at the fires, watching, alert to every movement, every twitch of the grasses, every rolling can, every stray plume of smoke that caught his eye. He was maintaining a vigilant watch, sure as he was that she was still around somewhere, that she hadn't escaped.

Sarah had learned the stranger's name: Graffiti. Several people knew him and addressed him by name. And their words drifted across to her alert ears. He scarcely acknowledged any greetings, sometimes inclining his head almost imperceptibly, sometimes doing nothing at all. That was until two others approached who obviously knew him well. The three of them stood together, while Graffiti filled them in on recent happenings. They looked in her direction when Graffiti indicated the end of the tunnel. They stood close together, their shoulders hunched, listening to his words, glancing up at his face, their expressions changing from serious and attentive to angry and determined. Sarah watched them and felt a chill creeping through her bones, knowing well that there were now three people searching for her.

All the while he spoke, Graffiti's eyes never stopped moving about, flickering towards every movement, peering into the shadows, trying to see across the yards of blackness to pick her out, find out where she was hiding. And his cronies picked up on his actions and began the same intense scouring of the area. Not only that, but she watched with dread as he dispatched them in her direction, to search the undergrowth for her, or to locate Flea. Maybe they were going to finish him off – or bury his body. Sarah wasn't sure of their reasons, but she shrank further into her stinking hole and listened intently while their footsteps crashed through the rubbish and weeds, their voices shouting to each other. Their search continued for a long time.

She didn't move and eventually their footsteps receded, their voices faded and she was alone again.

Sarah sensed a bleakness settle over her, an awful greyness that suffocated her in its cold bosom, a hopelessness about her situation. Her eyes were heavy and burning, her nerves twitching and raw. She was perished with the cold and her legs felt cramped. She rocked incessantly to and fro, trying to calm her jitters. Her thoughts raced.

She was worried about Flea, lying in the grass.

She was more worried about herself. The strangers scared her. Graffiti especially. He scared her like nothing had ever scared her before in her whole life. Not a shiver-up-your-spine-scared like you get when watching horror films or thrillers. That was fun – a run-out-of-the-room-and-hide type of fear that made you shriek and leap off the sofa and switch off the telly.

This was different.

Very different.

This was a corroding fear that ate at her thoughts and drove her frantic with the mind-blowing intensity of it. She was in danger. Real danger. Like she'd never been in before. This guy was crazy. Some drug-dealing lunatic who'd coolly stuck a knife in Flea and wouldn't hesitate to do the same to her. And he had crazy companions who were carrying out his lethal orders. And there was nothing she could do about it. Nothing except sit and wait like some cornered badger during the badger-baiting season.

She peeked out again and saw that his scouts had returned. They stood for a while longer, talking and then, finally, unbelievably, Graffiti and his henchmen abandoned their watch and sauntered inside, hands in their pockets. Sarah watched them with disbelief, not believing they had given up.

She was suspicious.

Surely this was an act. Graffiti was hardly going to give up now after standing waiting for almost – she checked her watch – two hours. He was probably just at the entrance of the Sheds waiting for her, waiting to pounce. And so she stayed, sitting alone in the cold and dark, sometimes dozing off into fitful, neck-aching snoozes that lasted half a minute or so before she jerked awake with a start and a shiver, but mostly just sitting and staring bleakly out at the darkness, rocking, rocking, rocking all the time.

It was only when the day nudged itself with an aching greyness into the patches of sky at the ends of the tunnel that Sarah roused herself and crept out of her alcove. The oil barrels had been abandoned entirely now except for one couple who lay entangled around each other on the warm, burnt earth.

Sarah crawled stiffly to the sodden grass and sat numbly while feeling gradually returned to her limbs.

She looked about her, seeing for the first time the place where she had spent most of the night. Nothing was familiar, as she had seen none of it before. This place had been shown to her through another sense and now the sight of it was foreign. The distances were different than she had imagined, the fires were further away, the end of the tunnel just a short distance whereas it had felt like miles when she had stumbled through it in the darkness. Even directions took on a new route, a different bearing. The alcove – was that not opposite the fires? Surely the tunnel was straight as a die?

Sarah sat, confused and dazed. There was a dream-like, alien feeling about the night's events, an impression that everything had occured in another time, another place, to another person. Sarah felt detached, an objective observer. She also felt calmer. Her frantic fear receded with the darkness. Her thoughts were sluggish, deadened. It was as if the rush of adrenalin she had been hyped up on all night had suddenly drained out of her veins and she was now limp, with no resources left to even think properly. She found that she could no longer clearly sequence in her own mind what had happened. In fact, had anything happened at all?

Dopily, she stood up, wincing with the pain of her stiff muscles. One knee was tender and hot to the touch. Feeling it gingerly, Sarah wondered what had happened to it. She felt miserable. Her head throbbed and her stomach felt awful.

Turning towards the tunnel entrance, she took a few steps, and then suddenly remembered Flea, lying half-dead at the other end of the building. Turning once again, she moved towards the tunnel end, stumbling unsteadily through the grass and junk that she could now at least see well enough to step over or around.

At the end of the tunnel where the broad wastelands spread out before her, Sarah squinted in the light of the drizzling dawn. She leaned against the wall and took several deep breaths of fresh air to fill her lungs with the morning and to brace herself for the possible sight of a dead Flea slumped against the brickwork.

Slowly, she swivelled her head and looked to where Flea and Graffiti had been arguing the night before. The long grass rippled in the breeze. Discarded papers and dirty tissues fluttered around, snagging against brambles and long grasses. Patches of soil, glimpsed between the tufts of grass and weeds, were burnt black from fires of other parties, other nights out. Rough circles of rocks indicated that the revellers had attempted to enclose their fires in some primitive hearth arrangement. Twisted beer cans and broken bottles littered the area.

But there was no sign of Flea.

Sarah stared. She stepped over the long grass to where she had seen the argument and the stabbing. Had her eyes been deceiving her? Was this where she had seen it? She looked around quickly. Maybe the distance and direction were deceptive in the darkness of the night and after the drinks she'd had. Perhaps Flea was against another wall, at some other part of the building, waiting to be found. Sarah moved away from the wall, out on to the wasteland, and scanned the length of the warehouse. Not a soul moved. All was quiet except for the eerie whispering of the caressing grasses. A fine mist was falling, swirling through the air and clinging to Sarah's hair, forming fine, shimmering cobwebs. She walked back to the spot where she had watched Graffiti plunge the knife into Flea. She tried to gauge the distance, attempted to imagine the scene as she had witnessed it. Then she paced the distance to where she reckoned the fight must have occured. Bending down, Sarah touched the bare earth at that spot, trying to get a sense of the night's happenings, trying to feel a warmth, an energy, from the black soil. But the earth only felt damp and clammy. Lifting her hand, Sarah looked at her fingertips. Were the soft pads of her fingers stained a reddish-brown? She poked at the soil, rubbing harder this time, and examined her fingertips. Yes, there was no doubt about it. Her fingers were darkened with a reddish colouring. This was where Flea had lain, injured and bleeding. Surer now that she hadn't imagined it and that she was at the right place, Sarah looked around, her sharp eyes looking for clues to what had happened. The grass was crushed, bruised, with plenty of broken stalks at that point. The movements of feet had torn the soft ground, leaving little scuff marks.

But Flea was gone.

Sarah tried to work out what might have happened, slumping down on her knees as she did so.

Either he had managed to get himself out of there, which was a good sign because it meant he wasn't too badly injured; in which case, he would surely have made his way home – he would hardly have gone back into the Sheds to look for her with Graffiti hanging around somewhere, would he? Or else somebody had found him lying on the ground; and then, the possibilities were endless. Who that somebody was was crucial. Perhaps Graffiti had returned, or the other guy who had been with Flea and Graffiti earlier on that evening – but why? To see if Flea was still alive? To find out if Sarah had gone to help him and so catch two birds with the one stone? To finish him off completely? Hardly to give him the kiss of life, Sarah decided. Perhaps some of Flea's own friends had come to look for him. They may have found him and brought him to a hospital. They may have discovered him already dead and brought his body off somewhere. What did somebody do with dead bodies or injured people in this bleak, abandoned place? Sarah gazed around her, the cold wind making her eyes water. One thing was certain – she wasn't going back inside to find out where Flea was. She would be certain to bump into Graffiti and that was one meeting she was anxious to avoid.

All Sarah wanted to do right now was to curl up in her bed and sleep, sleep, sleep. She was beyond any more thought and reasoning. Her sole focus for the immediate moment was to get home and get some rest.

Peering across the broad meadow through the film of rain, she could just discern a road far in the distance. She could see tiny vehicles, their lights still on, moving along and decided it was probably the most sensible direction for her to head in order to find her way home. Slowly, she stood up again. Ducking her head to avoid the drops and hunching her shoulders to keep in a little warmth, Sarah began to make her way through the grassy wilderness towards the distant highway.

By the time she reached the Afandi's house, after tramping through the meadow, hitching for a while and walking again, it was almost midday. She still had no idea where she had spent the night and was now so exhausted that she felt physically ill. Letting herself in by the front door, she stared with utter weariness and pure hatred at the long flight of steps that led to her room. Just a little rest before the mammoth climb, she promised herself as she leaned against the newel post, her head resting on her arms. She closed her eyes blissfully, sleep coming as completely and quickly as if she was sinking into a feather bed. It was only when her arms slipped from their precarious position on the shiny post and she clattered with an almighty and embarrassing crash on to the floor that she awoke. Mrs Afandi shimmered out of her room in a haze of yellow sequined sari, her brown eyes round with surprise. Sarah blinked apologetically at her from the floor and struggled upstairs to her room.

Without bothering even to draw the curtains, take off her clothes or turn back the covers, she fell across her bed and dropped into an immediate and heavy slumber.

A loud crash followed by a scream rent her dreams and woke Sarah, shattering her slumber, smashing the peace of sleep. The scream was high-pitched and long, sending a crazed vibration of noise through the house.

Sarah sat up in her bed with a start, suddenly alert to the noise. She looked towards the window, hoping to get some indication of what time of day it was. The sky was thickening, either gathering the night into its arms or ripening for a humdinger of a storm. Either way, it looked glum.

Sarah rubbed her eyes hard, forcing them to stay open despite their insistence on closing again. She was awake, but confused, her body refusing to cooperate with her mind, her system unable to immediately respond to her need to be fully awake and listening.

What was happening?

Who was screaming?

She stayed sitting up, straining her ears to hear what the sudden commotion was about, allowing her body to catch up with her now alert mind. Her broken thoughts quickly reassembled themselves after the rudeness of sudden awakening. She shivered.

Glancing towards the window, she was mildly surprised to see a vague flickering of colour, a brightening of the heavy gloom that pressed against the glass. Indistinct shapes danced and leaped, throwing flashing shadows around her room. Curious now, Sarah went over to the window. Opening it wide, she peered out, looking down at the side of the house.

But the sight that met her eyes shocked her to the core.

The small patch of scanty grass that grew untidily at the side of the house was a mass of flickering, dancing, leaping, flashing flames. Tongues of fire – orange, red, yellow, green, blue – licked the side of the house leaving long snaking trails of black smoke. More smoke soared upwards, twisting and turning crazily as the wind caught it and tossed it around.

Even as Sarah watched, the window of the flat below hers shimmered dangerously like a bubble that is about to burst. Oily rainbows slithered across its shiny surface until, with an awful popping sound, it exploded from the heat, sending out shards of splintered glass like honed bullets. More screams and cries filled the air.

Above the roar of the fire and the screaming that reverberated all around, Sarah could hear the sirens of distant fire engines. Pulling herself back into her room, she hurriedly pulled on a jacket and ran out of the door, taking the stairs two at a time in her hurry to get out. On the granite steps huddled the six little Afandis with their mother, who carried the baby. Three other residents stood in stunned shock watching the blaze.

The sudden roar of a car engine revving into life attracted their attention at the same moment as the car – previously parked across the road – swerved towards them, its headlights glaring.

"It's a drunken driver. Get back inside," Sarah yelled, afraid that it was going to hit them all. She instinctively grabbed two of the children and pushed them into the doorway. What was happening? Had the world gone crazy? Never had so many terrifying things happened to her all in the space of twenty-four hours.

But at the last moment, the car braked, skidding to a halt in front of the steps without hitting anything. There was a moment of pure silence, a pause of a second or perhaps only a millionth of a second while the engine was switched off. But in that time, Sarah suddenly knew with a terrible fear that gripped her heart and chilled the blood in her veins that the driver of this swerving, crazy car was not some out-of-control drunken driver, but that he was somebody who was very much in control.

Somebody who knew what he was doing.

Somebody called Graffiti.

The thought suddenly flashed unprompted – into her head. Before she saw his thin, hard face. Before she met his intense, blue eyes. Sarah's realisation exploded with a physical force that felt like a punch to her stomach. She knew without seeing him, she knew without being called by him, she knew without being told.

She just knew.

At the very same moment that the awful knowledge tore to ribbons her curiosity and left her gasping in the grip of raw terror, she realised how the fire that now blazed viciously had started. It had been a malicious attack, staged by him, to smoke her out, to expose her to him.

He climbed out of the driver's seat now, slowly and coolly. The memory of his slow, deliberate movements the previous night flooded into Sarah's mind. Leaning across the roof of the car, he pointed at her, singling her out, identifying her as his target. His eyes narrowed. His voice was soft, honed to a lethal sharpness yet scarcely louder than a whisper. Even above the roar of the fire, his words breathed softly into her ears, twitching the tiny, fine hairs therein. He could do nothing to her there, in front of a group of others, with the fire engines hurtling up the street and people gathering all around to watch the action. He could do nothing but frighten her with his words.

But frighten her he did.

When he spoke, his every syllable nestled in danger, burrowed into the lethal potency of his threat.

"I'm coming for you. Don't forget. You won't get away from me."

Sarah whimpered like a tiny child, paralysed by fear. She didn't, couldn't, move from where she stood on the steps, half turned towards him, half turned away.

She froze.

His words were in her head, crawling in her ears, filling her mind, all round, everywhere and nowhere at once, circling and circling. She whimpered again, not knowing where she was or what she was hearing.

The only thing Sarah could do to get away from that hideous voice and those steely eyes was to run. And, suddenly, she found herself sprinting. Her feet pounded the concrete pavement. Her breath came in short, painful gasps. Her heart hammered against her breastbone.

But even as she ran, her fear caught up with her and was so great that it blinded her. Sarah no longer knew where she was running to nor what she was running from.

PART TWO

November 20

He's there. I can see him. He's in the crowd. Just next to the comic stand, where they sell chewing-gum and fresh-breath mints. He's going to get me. Oh Christ, he has his knife, silver and shiny. He's cleaned it now. Cleaned off all the blood. Flea's blood has been cleaned away.

But I can get away from him. I know where to hide. He doesn't like the tunnels. I hid in a tunnel before and he couldn't find me. All the long dark night I hid in the tunnel while he had to stand at the fire to stay warm. I didn't need to. Didn't need to stay warm. I can survive. I can hide. I'm smart. I can outwit him. I can get away from him. In the dark. On my own. With no fires.

I wish I could go home now. This is no fun anymore, but I'm so scared of that Graffiti. Suppose he gets to my parents? Suppose he knows where I'm from and how to find me. What if he harms my family, all because of me? What if it's my fault and he hurts them? They wouldn't know what to do. They don't even know about this kind of stuff happening, and even if they did, they wouldn't ever believe anybody could do such a thing to a sane, normal human being. I wouldn't have believed it myself except that it's happening to me.

I've no ticket home and no money to buy one. I could ring but what could my family do? They're miles away and even if they came over, I'd have to meet them at the airport and Graffiti would probably guess what was going on and be there too.

Could I be really that selfish? Am I such an awful person that I dump my family and run away when I feel I've had enough of them, but as soon as things get difficult, ring them for my own greedy reasons? Anyway, they wouldn't understand the urgency and panic of everything. They'd want to discuss it all and talk calm sense into me, but this is no time to start peace negotiations. Maybe I should ring and warn them – or would that be stupid?

November 21

I can't go back to the Afandi's because I know he's there – waiting for me. Lying in wait for me. In the burnt house. In the blackened, charred, Graffiti-incinerated house that I used to live in. He's in *my* room with *my* clothes and *my* belongings. He's looking in *my* bathroom at *my* toiletries. He's rummaging through *my* clean shirts and jumpers. He's fingering through the pages of *my* passport. I hate this. I hate this. I have to stay out, out in the open. Then I can see him coming. I know he won't catch me when I'm outside. It's too cold for him.

I've no money except the few quid I had in my pocket from the party in the Sheds. Enough for a taxi and a few drinks, but that's it. All my money from working with Bakhtiar is in the post office and my savings book is in the house. Or more likely in Graffiti's pocket by this stage. I'll have to get some money from somewhere. I'll have to eat to keep alive on these foul, greasy streets and in the dirty, dusty tube-stations.

I am sore with running. My muscles are sore and stiff. Stiff with the cold too. My stomach cramps and pains me with the fear of knowing Graffiti's after me. Oh God, oh God, how can I escape from the pain and the fear and *him* and I have to sleep and I can't sleep and I'm out on the streets and it's raining and blowing and dark and nobody is around except drunks and punks and savages. I stole some pizza slices today from one of the stands at Leicester Square and ran, ran, ran until nobody was shouting at me anymore. My heart thudded and hurt and my stomach hurt, but I was starving with the hunger and I have to eat.

I want to go home now more than anything else. I'm terribly homesick and it's like some corroding disease inside me that's eating all my thoughts up so all I have left inside my head is sheer panic and a desperate need to go home. But I've resolved not to – for now. I can't go running home as soon as things turn sour. I'm made of stronger stuff than that and I don't want Dad and Clem and Mum and Alice to see me as a dejected, frightened, filthy coward. I have to hang on. I have to show I'm able to manage. That I can deal with this. I won't be beaten by some knife-wielding creep. I can survive. I'm a survivor – remember. I'll show them I can manage on my own, my own life. My own living. On my own terms.

November 22

He's all around. He manages to get everywhere. Now he's over there. He's just there behind me. He creeps towards me with his knife. Aaaaah! Graffiti. Graffiti. He stalks me in my dreams and inhabits my nightmares. I can't sleep. I can't sleep any more, anywhere, or else he'll get me. He knows how to climb into my dreams and seep into my mind. Graffiti. My skin seethes with him beneath it. He writhes inside my brain.

I have to run from him, run into the tunnels to escape from him for a little while. Until they put me out. The guards put me out. At half past two in the morning, they put me out on the streets just so he can get me.

He'll get me.

He'll get me.

Run, Sarah, run!

It's cold outside. Freezing cold that clings to your skin and hair and ears and eyelashes and fingers and toes and nose. I'm freezing. Shivering, shivering, shivering, but it's the only way to escape, for he likes the fires. He likes the warmth of the fires, so if I stay out in the cold, he can't get me.

November 24

I rang home today, rang my own home number and heard the voice of Alice. She answered the phone. But I didn't speak. I didn't say anything, just listened and listened while my money ran through and tears ran down my face and Alice asked again and again "Who's there? Who's there? Hello?" I wanted to hear their voices, hear them say "hello" but not to hear me. If they heard me, they'd know I couldn't manage. So they're not allowed to hear me. Can't let them know it's difficult. Hard to manage on your own. Not so easy after all. After my change had run through, I just sat on the ground under the phone and blubbered like some big baby. I have never wanted my family and my home and my Mum so much in my entire life, but at the same time, I have never been more determined to hang on and sit it out and prove to myself as well as them that I can manage.

The tunnels are warm and I know there's safety here, safety from him, even though it's not cold. I can ride the rats from station to station and never get caught, being too smart for the guards. Too smart for Graffiti. I don't need to run fast now. The rats are on my side. They weren't always. Their lairs used to be too dark and deep for me, but now they're not. They're safe and warm and Graffiti is never here. I can rat-ride all day long and know he won't find me. I don't have to run when I'm rat-riding.

Can't sleep still. Can't sleep. Can't sleep. He's in my dreams still. He's there in my dreams, in my nightmares, with his knife. His knife is sharp and polished. I can see it when I close my eyes. Flames dance along the edge of it. Moonbeams live on the surface of it. Flea's face screams from the flash of steel. It slices through the air. Coming towards me. Forever? Always? Coming towards me.

November 25

I met someone today. I think it was one of his men. One of Graffiti's men out to find me. To get me. Today. One of his people. Working for him like the guards. I was sitting in the tunnel, waiting for the rush of hot wind that tells you when one of the underground rats is coming. You don't need to see them or hear them to tell they're on their way. They just blow their hot, fume-laden breath all the length of the tunnel and then you know they're coming. They grumble and rumble and scurry loudly out of their lairs to slide along next to you.

Anyway, this guy sits next to me. He's rubbing up really close. His knee brushes against mine. His shoulder nudges me. Chummy-like. He smiles, but a hard, brittle smile. Then he asks me my name.

But I'm clever. Too clever for that stuff, remember? I'm a survivor.

"Annie," I tell him.

"Yeah? Annie what?"

"Annie name you want but my real one," I pipe up, all bright and smart. Grinning from ear to ear. Graffiti's men can't outwit me.

He's not too impressed, though. He starts talking all rough and coarse. Lewd words. Dirty suggestions. He grabs my knee and pulls it towards him, so I kick him really hard in the shins and yell. I ran then. Ran really fast from that tunnel so that he couldn't get me. Had to crawl under one of the turnstiles to get out. Had this big black guard shouting at me. Yelling at me to come back. But I didn't. I kept running. Sarah kept running. To get away. To escape.

It scared me. Scared me half to death. It was a close shave. Graffiti could have had me there. Could have got me good and proper. It took me a long time to calm down. I was jittery all day, checking everyone who sat within an ass's roar of me. Jumping up and running on if I didn't like the look of them, or if they looked twice at me.

November 28

This old guy gave me money. Left it on the ground in front of me. I was sitting checking out the feet to see if I'd recognise Graffiti's if he came into the tunnels. You have to keep checking the feet. Can't look up at the eyes. Can't look up at the faces. Otherwise, they'll see you and look down. They don't like that. The passers-by don't expect you to be looking up when you're sitting way down there at their feet, so you have to keep looking down. It scares them when they see you looking straight up at them, meeting their eyes from your way-down place. So you toe the line and watch the feet instead. I reckon I'd recognise Graffiti's feet from the slow, cool way he'd pause and then approach. Oh no, oh no, it scares me. Don't think of it. Don't think of him, Sarah. He scares me. If he comes for me I'll die. Like Flea. Like poor, dead, cold Flea.

Stop. Stop it. Move on, move on. You'll manage. You'll survive. You're a survivor.

The money – I let it sit there for ages. I was watching it for a long time, just to be sure. In case it was a plant, you know? Might have been a set-up. One of his people

– like before. You can't be too careful in this day and age. Have to watch your back all the time. Especially with Graffiti out to get you with his knife.

Anyway, after an hour or so, I reckoned it was safe enough so I took it. Went to the nearest MacDonald's and ordered a Big Mac meal. I ate it all so, so slowly and deliciously, savouring each hot, salty, delectable, crispy french fry and each mouthful of warm, pickly, juicy, dripping, cheesy, meaty burger until I felt full. Never before has food tasted so wonderful and necessary and essential and delicious. I could feel the warmth creep slowly through all of me until my arms and legs were aching with life. And my stomach wasn't hurting too much either.

December 1

She kind of looked a bit crazy, sitting there all screwed up in a little dried-up ball like some sort of cow-turd. Her hair was cow-turd coloured too and you couldn't see her eyes because they kept looking down at the ground all the time. Probably didn't make any difference – I knew they'd be turdy too. She'd been sitting there for ages, ravelling and unravelling this little, scutty piece of silky twine round her index finger.

The only reason I noticed her was that she'd taken up my spot. My favourite spot between the two long escalators that go down, down, down or up, up, up, depending on the way you're travelling. I like that spot best in the whole place because you can see who's coming down and who's coming up at the same time.

Then, if the feet of someone threatening come along, you still have a whole escalator to escape on because you're only halfway to anywhere, being between two escalators.

The significance of the spot was wasted on Turdy, however, because she just spent her whole time looking at her bit of string. She could do that anywhere. She didn't need to take up my spot to do it.

I have to find another vantage point. Ruins my day. Can't stay there now. Can't stay and wait. Don't like anywhere else so much. Nowhere else is as safe. Can't settle all day. Can't settle to feet-watching or rat-riding for the whole long day. What if she's working for Graffiti? What if she's one of them? Out to get me. Have to spend the whole day running and hiding, running and hiding.

All because of Turdy.

December 2

"Jerusalem Cold Weather Project"

It's written above the door in big white painted letters. On the inside of the glass like the window of a butcher's shop where the day's specials are written up. The first two and a half words look good, straight and even, but whoever painted it didn't leave themselves enough room so that " . . . her Project" is all squashed and crooked.

I came along to have a look at it early on today. Check it out. See what's going down in this place. A hostel, they call it. I saw it advertised on this little card stuck against the glass in a telephone booth in the station – a freephone number and the address; the works, you know, so it costs nothing to contact them. They give you a hot shower and a good dinner. Might help me shake this rotten cold with stuffed head and aching chest and runny nose that's been dragging out of me for nearly a week now. Maybe I'll give this place a shot tonight.

Later

It's three in the morning. I can't sleep in this crackpot place. Too many weirdos here, all round me. Maybe it's me. Maybe I'm the crackpot. I haven't slept in a bed for ages. Jesus, I can't even remember when. I've got so used to kipping somewhere, anywhere, in the day or night and jumping up as soon as some old creep comes up or the guards in the stations move me on. I'm writing now by the light of the hall lamp that shines in the open door. It's too hot here. Hot and stuffy and closed-in. It's fresher outside. Fresher and easier to breathe. The room smells and I am scared of these weird women who are sleeping all around me. They snore and rattle and sigh and snort and slurp and heave and rock and swallow and scratch and gulp and curse in their sleep so that the room sounds like a herd of cattle have settled for the night.

It's a right old melting-pot too of every old hobo and wino and druggie and vagrant and down-and-out and whore that ever walked the streets of London. And me stuck in the middle of the lot of them – just great!

December 3

I got half a night's sleep last night in the end. One of the staff, Rosie, gave me some Lemsip for my stuffed head and told me to make sure and not sleep out tonight or else it'd get worse and go into my chest. She talked to me for ages and I told her some of the things that are happening to me. (To tell the truth, I was half scared to tell her everything in case she knew Graffiti, so I left out a big chunk.) I cried a bit too and she hugged me and I felt a lot better after talking to her. She's going to give me some money tomorrow to tide me over for a while, and said that I shouldn't feel bad about ringing my family when things are down. She said they'd be so delighted to hear from me that they wouldn't notice I was only ringing to cheer myself up.

Today's all sunny and frosty and cold. Everything is flashing bright from the low white sun and not once did I see Graffiti hanging round any corners waiting for me. This is a good day. I must have shaken him off. Staying in that place has thrown him off the scent for a while. Nobody was at my spot between the escalators either. I walked through the park and had a swing on the swings. It's beautiful today and I feel happy. And I can do anything I want. I can go anywhere and meet anyone and stay anywhere.

It got cold in the evening so that my ears and my fingers and my nose turned red and and were singing from the wind. I've been outside all day and feel fresh. When the darkness closed in, I went to the loo in the train station to warm up under the hand-drier, but a fat Indian woman in a blue nylon coat told me to get out.

I'm going to stay in the project again tonight.

December 5

The deli is shut. Grey metal shutters seal up the front of it; floor-to-ceiling curtains of steel. Impenetrable. All-knowing. Not telling. Locking in its secrets. Locking out its visitors.

Where is Bakhtiar?

I rattled the shutters. I kicked at the lock. Nobody answered my yells, except a curious cat who wandered out from a back alley. No Bakhtiar. No Flea. No deli. No sandwich bar.

Nothing.

December 7

Guess who I discovered in the Project tonight – sleeping in the bed right next to mine? Turdy! When I came back from getting food, there she was, sitting all dried-up on her little bed dangling her little piece of string between her fingers, eyes down, head bent. I almost said "Hiya, Turdy," straight away because it was like meeting someone I knew but luckily, I remembered that's not her name and just said "Hi" instead. She said nothing. Just sat there. But I saw her eyes flicker towards me for an instant and I knew she saw me.

December 9

Rosie's the boss woman in the project. She's in charge of who gets into the project every night and she checks everyone through her little TV monitor before unlocking the doors and letting them in. She wanders round the rooms then and chats to people once she's taken names for the forms. She's dead nice, all warm and chatty. She's worked in the project for seven years and knows all the regulars. She introduced me to blind Catho. Catho is about ninety and all shrivelled up and has funny crooked feet that point in the wrong direction so that her boots look like she's put them on back-to-front and wrong-way-round. She's not really blind at all because, after meeting me, she yelled at me to bring her more soup – and that was when I was halfway across the canteen – so her sight can't be that bad.

I'm really glad I was in tonight, because outside it blew and rained and sleeted and hailed and froze all over the place. Wonder where little sad Turdy with her silky twine was staying tonight? She wasn't in the project, and nobody had seen her for a couple of days. I checked out all the rooms and the toilets and the showers and the canteen and the kitchen, but I couldn't find her. I even checked twice with Rosie because sometimes if somebody's sick or beaten up or drunk, she'll move them into another room she has with just two beds in it at the back of the office.

But Turdy wasn't there.
I hope she's OK.

December 10

Tonight was funny and kind of nice too.

I stayed in the project and hogged the bed next to the window. It's the best bed because you can open the window and breathe the night air and look out at the sky and turn your back on all the other people in the room and pretend you're anywhere else you want to be except in a hard bed with disinfected sheets in a smelly room in the Cold Weather Project with a million people who've damn all other places to go. You have to be smart to get the bed next to the window, though. Any new person wanders round and checks out the beds, so it's easy to get the jump on them. But the regulars like blind Catho gallop straight for the good beds and grab them, so you've to be on the ball. I'm telling you, Catho's crooked feet and blind eyes never stop her nabbing the best bed in the room once Rosie's filled in her form for her. You have to be at the doors early and fill up your form fast, fast, fast so that you can grab your blanket and towel and run up to the rooms ahead of the others.

Anyway, on the empty bed next to mine was a familiar little piece of string, all wound up in a scruffy ball. I knew it immediately and lay down on my own bed to wait. Sure enough, after a few minutes, Turdy trotted along and sat up on the bed, her short little legs swinging away, her busy fingers picking up her string and winding, unwinding, winding, unwinding for ages and ages, her eyes flickering towards me, away from me, towards me, away from me.

I said nothing to her because she knew I was there

122

and I could see her expression. A ghost of a smile was tickling her lips now and then, shivering across her face for an instant or two and then vanishing. But she kept sitting there, swinging her legs and twisting her string and flickering her eyes. I knew what she was up to. Knew she was talking to me but she wasn't using words. Knew she was dancing round in conversation. She was playing games with me. She was dipping in and out of wordless chatter, while I waited and listened and watched.

It was fun, and I smiled too.

After food and a shower, I lay on the bed in the darkness and smelt the Dettol in the sheets and pillows. In the softness of the night, Turdy began talking. At first, I didn't even notice that she'd started using words. All night she had played games with me – glancing at me, giving me her piece of string, then snatching it back again, touching the sleeve of my jacket, resting her gaze on me for a few moments, sitting next to me in the canteen, placing half her sausage on my plate and, in turn, taking half of my sausage. Her presence was like words and sentences. Her movements told me stories. Her expressions described her thoughts. Voiceless words had been coming from her all evening, so that when she actually began to talk, I didn't register the change. Her voice, when it came, was whispery and high.

When I finally tuned in, her words were meaningless to me, senseless sounds that dipped and peaked like real speech, but meant nothing. Her words were empty of sense, guttural sounds mingled with snatches of children's rhymes and fairytales, the words of pop songs and chart hits, snippets of maths tables and poems that reminded me of school. She sang a little and whimpered a little, laughed harshly like a magpie and sobbed so suddenly and savagely that I sat up and stared at her in fright.

She looked at me then, suddenly silent and serious, her eyes wide and shining roundly in the light from the hall. She turned over in her bed and closed her eyes and I did the same.

December 13

Turdy never shuts her face. All day long she trips along beside me, chirruping and singing and sobbing and muttering in her garbled string of nonsense that's driving me up the bloody wall. I wouldn't mind if I could understand what the hell she's talking about, because she's forever pointing stuff out and looking at things and showing me bits of string that she's found. She gets all excited about bits of string – especially coloured ones or ones made up of three or four threads of different colours that you find at the embroidery counters of department stores. Sends her into some kind of frenzy and she goes hopping around and pulling at my jumper and yelping excitedly like a six-month-old puppy. When she shows me stuff, she warbles and chatters like some kind of drunk sparrow and her voice goes up and down like normal talking, but it's just strings of words. Garbage. Rubbish. Nonsense.

And it drives me crazy. Why can't she just talk?

December 15

We went to the theatre tonight. No kidding. The real live theatre. I haven't been to the theatre in yonks. It was brilliant. We were hanging around outside the *Barbican* where there was some big production on. At the interval, the audience poured out to the bars and the lobby, chatting and gathering into little groups to discuss the plot and study their programmes. So Turdy and I made our move. We held our heads up high and without looking left or right, we strutted straight through the crowds and into the auditorium. Nobody checks theatre tickets at the interval and the staff were so busy serving drinks and ushering people to their drinks tables that nobody looked twice at us. We sneaked into two seats way up high, right at the back. There were no coats or bags near the seats and we waited while the interval was on and then everyone poured back to watch the rest of the performance.

The lights went down. The curtain lifted. Nobody tried to claim our seats. We were in ancient Rome, with slaves and chariots and dancing girls. There were sparks and smoke that came shooting through gas jets on the stage, and swirls of orange fire and strobe lighting. People were born and lived their whole lives and got murdered, all on stage in front of us. Armies went to war and rioted and rampaged. Countries were taken and kings were dethroned. We never found out the name of the play or really got to grips with the storyline because we had missed the first half, but it was great.

We're going to do it again next week.

December 16

"You know the rules, girls. First come, first served," Rosie yelled through her intercom, her voice crackling with static. We couldn't get into the project – even the two emergency beds behind the office were full. She'd no space for us. It was the time of year. Every old hobo comes out of the woodwork to stay in the project round Christmas-time. Turdy yelled really loud at Rosie, shouting and kicking the door and hammering on it with her fists. Rosie handed us out some buns and burgers. She also gave us two mugs of tea but Turdy was mad at her and threw the mugs against the door, smashing them. She could have done it to her own tea, but she didn't have to do it to mine. I got no tea just because she was so mad. She tried to grab at Rosie too. Tried to grab her hair with her angry fists. That was a stupid thing to do. Rosie was mad then. She barred Turdy for two nights for bad behaviour. Great. Two nights with no shelter all because Turdy got so angry. I couldn't just leave her and go into the project on my own tomorrow night or the next, so there were two of us out for two nights.

December 17

Turdy's asleep on the floor of this house. It's on a building site and it's new. The back door had a glass panel with soft putty so we picked it off and crawled through. I like the smell of new, damp putty, an aniseed smell. I rolled together a little ball of it to rub between my fingers and sniff. We found broken boxes and lit them in the back room to make a fire, then we drank some whiskey from a bottle Turdy had lifted from some shop earlier on.

It was a good thing for me, but it wasn't such a good thing for Turdy. It made me feel all floaty and free and warm and liquidy, but it didn't do the same to her. All kinds of thoughts pop into your mind when you're sitting in the dark in front of a spitting fire and drinking whiskey. Turdy got miserable. Thinking whiskey-painted thoughts always makes her sad. It's not a hard thing for her to get sad though, because she spends lots of time during the day sobbing and whimpering, but this was worse than that. She was bawling – big heaving sobs that shook her and made her breath catch. I had to hold on to her, like a baby. She was just a little kid made of bones and I was hanging on to her and she was crying.

She started talking too. *Real* talking. Proper words, not garbled gibberish. She can talk, but won't tell me why she doesn't. She sings her words like a little bird, but I could understand them. Once she got going, it was hard to stop her. She started telling me all about her family and why she left home. Scarey stuff about her parents divorcing and her mum moving in with this new guy who fancied Turdy like mad. He's a white guy and big with a hairy moustache and hairy hands (she kept on about his hairy hands), while Turdy's small and brown and kind of weak-looking. He wouldn't leave her alone, groping and touching and feeling her. He'd follow her around the house when they were alone and do stuff to her, hurt her. She tried telling her mum, but her mum wouldn't believe her and told her not to be jealous and acting spoilt. Can you believe that? Not to be jealous of some old creep who would mess her around as soon as they were alone. This went on for a while, but then Turdy got sick of it. She was afraid he'd make her pregnant.

So she ran away.

She left. Left and ran, ran, ran. That was weeks ago and she hasn't been home since. Hasn't rung or written. Hasn't called or visited. She still gets scared and trembly when she thinks of her mother's new boyfriend. She even got frightened talking to me. After telling me all about him, she curled up into a tight little ball and rocked herself to and fro, to and fro, on the concrete floor, twisting a little piece of string and whimpering rubbish to herself. I didn't like seeing her do that. It scared me. She looked crazy. All twisted and baby-like and talking to herself. She's just a mess – and she didn't even do it herself. At least if I'm a mess, I did it to myself and I've no one else to blame.

Turdy fell asleep in the end, so now I'm just hanging on in the darkness of this empty house until she wakes up. Her words disturbed me so much that I can't sleep. I'm just sitting with my back against the wall, writing by the light of the orange streetlamp. Hanging on and thinking, thinking, thinking.

December 18

It's better sitting round this fire than sitting in a corner at the station or lying on the floor of an empty house while Turdy rocks crazily beside me. An old guy in the corner, with his feet in an empty box of Cyprus oranges, is singing some old song about a sailor gone to sea who had to leave his sweetheart behind. His voice keeps cracking. Cracking up and down and high-pitched and low-pitched, wobbling and shaking. He sounds like he's crying.

Maybe he *is* crying.

Maybe this old guy is crying because the song is sad. I feel like crying too. Crying because I'm sad. Not because of some lousy old sad song about a sailor, but because I'm sad for Turdy and cold for myself. Come to think of it, I'm freezing. My arse is freezing off on the concrete, even though I have a flattened box under me and a blanket wrapped round me.

Eight of us are sitting round this tea-crate fire and we're staring like zombies into the flames. We're all listening to the cracking, splintered voice of the old boy in the Cyprus orange box and I think everyone's sad for everything else except the poor sailor. We're drinking from a bottle that's being handed round by a boy with only one eye. It's a gin bottle but the stuff inside is brown and has a funny taste, so maybe it's not gin at all. Turdy is leaning against me and her bony shoulder is warm and comforting. Her nose is running, so she keeps giving great big sniffs and I can feel her moving against me. We got hot food earlier on from these people in a van who drove over and handed out soup and rolls and coffee. We also got given the blanket and I took some aspirin because my head is splitting.

December 19

After the fires went out and the air got cold again and my face wasn't burning from the flames, the one-eyed boy came over. I could smell his boozey breath and the street from his coat. He had a wad of dirty cotton wool stuck over his gammy eye and the other one peered at us closely, all bloodshot and watery. I got a fright first because I thought suddenly he was with Graffiti, but it turned out he wasn't. Said he'd never heard of anyone called Graffiti, but he seemed to know Turdy. Or at least, he'd seen her around before. He asked us where we were staying because he'd a room not far from the fire that was warm and dry. He said we could stay there if we wanted. It sounded good. I was sleepy and didn't want to get any colder. My head was throbbing and I felt like I did the night I was at the party with Flea. (Was that really only a month ago? It feels like it was light years away and that I've lived a whole lifetime since then.) I just want to sleep, sleep, sleep.

The old boy in the orange box had either gone to sleep or died. He was slumped over, dribbling on to his chest, and he wasn't singing any more. Some of the others had wandered off or else gone to sleep in their boxes and blankets, curled near the blackened fire.

Turdy and me decided to take our chances with Popeye.

It turned out that his room was in a lousy dump of a derelict building on the edge of a football pitch. We had to climb through a cellar door in the back of the house and crawl over heaps of junk before coming out to a kitchen where the floor was slimy. It was pitch black and smelt like rotten cabbages, but Pop-eye used a cigarette lighter to show us the way. He started joking first by flickering it under his chin so that in the glimmering light, he was all spooky and scary. But he singed his stubble and gave a yell. He decided it wasn't funny after that.

We went upstairs, from where we could hear voices.

He opened this door of a room at the back and suddenly we weren't in a smelly, dark, dank old building any more. We were in a room with two other young people who were chatting and drinking and lying around. It was warm and candles stuck in empty beer bottles burned everywhere, making the room smell of wax and flicker first dark, then bright, then dark again.

Anyway, we sat around for a while just listening and warming up. They were all smoking and Turdy and Pop-eye lit up too, but I don't smoke. I drank a bottle of beer instead that this girl gave to me. They started asking us about ourselves and where we had come from. They couldn't believe that we weren't on some kind of income from the social services people. Tomorrow we're going to get signed on for social service money. Pop-eye gave us a rundown on the kind of questions we might be asked and the answers we were to give. It was late when we finally blew out the candles and lay down on some unzipped sleeping bags to sleep.

December 21

Pop-eye and his friends are just great. They brought us down to social services yesterday and, after a grilling interview, this sour-faced man who spends his days pen-pushing behind a desk, and obviously hates his job, reluctantly agreed to give us a regular payment. Turdy had to lie about her age and tell them she was over sixteen, while I had to say I had moved over to London from Dublin with my family. We also gave false addresses, but it doesn't matter. From Friday on, we'll get money into our sweaty little fists to spend as we like! We also just got registered in time to benefit from the Christmas bonus, so we'll get extra. It's just so brilliant. I don't know why I didn't do all this months ago, but I suppose I knew nothing about it and I had this fear at the back of my mind that somebody would catch me out, find out that I had run away from home and frogmarch me back to Dublin.

We're staying in Pop-eye's house for a while too because it's fun, fun, fun and the others are really friendly. It's not really his house at all; it was just an empty house he broke into one day with his brother, Mickey. They found one room that didn't have soggy floorboards and a funny grey mould with black speckles growing all over the walls, and so they stayed there. The other rooms upstairs aren't safe to walk in because the floors are sagging, but downstairs is fine. You can't really use the toilet because the water has been shut off and the room is very smelly, but there is a cold-water tap outside the cellar door.

Turdy is so excited about this place and keeps switching excitedly between her sparrow-talk and her rubbishy singing. At least she hasn't been sobbing for a while.

December 23

We're decorating the room in the house for Christmas. Sattar, Mickey's girlfriend, came in today with a huge armful of fresh green holly and we spent ages draping it around the window frames and hanging it from the ceiling. Pop-eye got some spray paints in gold and silver and red, and we sprayed Christmas messages all over the walls and the stairs and the doors until the place was bright and seasonal. We also sprayed all the empty beer bottles and candles. The smell of the spray paints made me feel sick and headachy so we left for a couple of hours while it dried off.

December 24

Today Turdy and me got our first payments so we went on a bus tour of London. We ate out in *Paolo's Pizza* with an "as-much-as-you-can-eat-for-a-fiver" offer. We stuffed ourselves until we were nearly sick and then we went window-shopping.

The shops are really pretty with tinsel and holly and Santas and presents and cards. They smell of wax and new leather and rich food and warm heat. We wandered round the toy department and the place where they sell the decorations. It's all so lovely. I've never before wandered round the shops on Christmas Eve with nothing special to buy. Usually, I've a hundred presents to get and masses of cards to buy and everything is sold out because I've left it too late so I end up charging round like a headless chicken and grabbing any old gift at all. This was different. I could spend the time watching lots of other headless chickens instead.

Turdy chattered and touched all the sparkling baubles and glittering strings of beads. She cried a little when she smelt the handmade chocolates and fingered the crib figures, but overall, we had a good day. I was so tired when I went to bed that I could hardly wait for my head to touch the sleeping bag, and in a way I was glad I was so tired because what with all the lovely Christmassy stuff and holly and decorations and what with it being Christmas Eve, I'm thinking about home again . . .

I'd like maybe to go home after Christmas and share some of the sacred, blessed season with my own family. I think too I'm past the worst of my scary time with Graffiti – he's probably gone to ground by now and has forgotten about chasing me. Going home would still be selfish but not so bad because I don't need rescuing any more. I've survived and one tiny part of me can almost admit to being happy.

December 25

Christmas day! I can hardly believe I'm spending Christmas morning in a sleeping bag on the floor of a derelict house in London. I feel I've been cheated out of Christmas and I've only myself to blame.

This afternoon, we're all going to the *Jerusalem Cold Weather Project* for our Christmas dinners. We signed our names on yesterday and we have to be there at half past twelve.

Later

We've had defrosted turkey roll with roasters and stuffing and I'm bursting at the seams. It's great. Turdy and I are sitting in front of the telly in the big sitting-room. Pop-eye and Mickey and Sattar left after dinner, so maybe we'll see them later, or maybe we won't if we decide to stay here the night. The way I'm feeling now, I can't move an inch and won't be able to for an hour yet!

Later on, I'm going to ring home. I was talking to Rosie about it and she'll give me the money, but I'm already so nervous that I wish I hadn't eaten so much.

December 26

I rang home last night and listened and waited while Clem answered and spoke and waited and listened. My money chinked through and suddenly Clem said, "Sarah? Is that you?" I couldn't take that. It gave me a scare and it upset me at the same time. Imagine that he knew. He knew straight away it was me. He sensed I was listening and breathing at the other end of the line. Then we were all talking and crying at the same time. Dad was on the extension upstairs and Mum was shouting on the downstairs phone. They wanted me to come home at once. They wanted to send me money and tickets, to come and collect me in person. They knew I'd been working in Bakhtiar's deli, and that I'd been living at the Afandi's. How did they know all this? Who had told them where I'd been and what I'd been up to? I mean, I hadn't even been in touch since leaving home, so they didn't get all the news from me. I felt a bit bewildered by it all. It was suddenly happening too fast. Suddenly racing along and happening without me deciding the pace. I was abruptly flung on to a wild out-of-control roundabout that was spinning and making me feel sick. Mum even said they'd received my rucksack and clothes and papers from the police and were worried sick about where I was living now. They wanted my new address – where was I? Who was I staying with? They even wanted to know what I was wearing, for Chrissakes.

I didn't want things to go out of my control like this once I had made the call. I didn't want them to know all about me before I had a chance to give them the news myself.

After I put the phone down, I was upset. Not because I was sad or homesick or lonely, but because suddenly I didn't want to talk to them any more. I had rung and talked and wished them season's greetings, but they knew *everything* about me already. It made me so mad. When am I ever going to get a bit of privacy to do my own thing? Anyway, how did they find out all these things?

I needed time to think. To work things out. To decide what the next step would be. I didn't want them to seize the reins and direct the horses just because I had made a call. There would be so much I'd have to explain and justify and answer. I don't know if I'm ready for all that. Not all the third degree. I don't want the drag of questions and great reunions and travelling home to Dublin.

December 27

Turdy may go home. Not to her own home, but maybe she'll go somewhere that'll help her. A social worker that Rosie called has been talking to her all evening.

Later

Turdy's been whispering to me in the dark. In the dark, in the hostel, about what we're going to do. She doesn't want to go anywhere till I'm sorted out, then maybe she'll see. The social worker's coming back tomorrow, but Turdy's not going to be there – not tomorrow. We're sticking together. She has the social worker's number on a little piece of paper scrunched up in her pocket so she can ring her if she wants, but we won't be hanging round.

December 28

We left early on this morning, before seven-thirty, as soon as we got breakfast. It was still dark and the pavement was sparkling with frost. There was a stillness about, a holding of breath before the life of the day exhaled its frenzy and I felt like I had one up on the city, stealing around its streets while it still slept. I was privy to its intimate moments, a secret observer of its private time.

We had packed our pockets with rolls and jam and

bananas and left the *Jerusalem Cold Weather Project*. Turdy and me are going to sort out what happened to Flea. We went first to Bakhtiar's deli, but it's still all sealed up with metal shutters. The windows above had curtains closed on them. Perhaps it's too early for Bakhtiar to have opened up and we didn't knock. Later on, when the day has started and the city is in full frenzy, we'll come back and look for him – see what's been going on.

We walked around to the Afandi's house, but I couldn't go close. I felt sick and my throat hurt and my muscles jumped, so I stayed near the market square, softly crunching the film of ice on the top of a puddle with my toe, while Turdy went round to the house. She was back in a while, all grins and smiles and little hops. The house is all fixed up, new windows, fresh paint, no burnt mess. No sign of Graffiti.

Not today though. Not today. I can't go there today. Maybe tomorrow. Maybe I'll visit there tomorrow and speak to Mrs Afandi. We'll see. I won't promise anything.

Tonight I'll just think about it instead.

Later

In the afternoon, we headed back to Bakhtiar's deli. The place looked all shut up at first, but then I remembered – he was probably in the back eating his own lunch, listening to the radio and reading the papers like he always used to do. I rattled the door a bit and shouted out his name. Turdy twittered and hopped around. After a long time, he came shuffling in from the back room in his old slippers, giving out lingo, his face all grouchy-looking. But, wow, did he change when he saw me! All these great expressions flitted across his face like the shadows from clouds chasing across a windswept field. He opened the door and just stood there, looking at me.

"You're late," he snapped, and it was just like old times. Then, as he looked me up and down, "and you can't have you job back smelling and looking like you do."

We went in to the deli and had a feed of sandwiches and mugs of tea. And then we talked and talked, filling each other in on what had happened. Bakhtiar had had a rough few weeks when Flea and I just hadn't reappeared one morning.

"I'd have willingly strung you both from the rafters, if I could have laid my hands on you," he snapped, but I could tell he was over it now. He'd two new people working for him, and no, Flea hadn't been in touch, although Bakhtiar knew something serious had happened. The police had arrived a couple of days later, asking questions and checking out the deli, but offering no information. Bakhtiar listened in silence while I told him of Graffiti, of sleeping rough and of meeting Turdy. To my surprise, he knew of Graffiti and shook his head. His face tightened into an angry scowl, but he made no comment.

While we were talking, Turdy fell asleep on the sofa, snoring loudly. In the end, Bakhtiar agreed to let us sleep in the back room for the night, on condition we didn't nick any food from the deli. "But you're not coming back to work here," he told me on his way to bed. "You're too unreliable."

December 29

We left Bakhtiar's early this morning, full of hot sausage sandwiches and glad farewells. I think Bakhtiar was happy to know that I was still alive and kicking, but not sorry to see the back of me and Turdy.

After his warmth, Mrs Afandi's reception was another matter. At first, she didn't even know me. I had to tell her who I was. I had to show her my room, that I *knew* my room. Showed her that I knew my way all round her house. She kept looking at me. Peering at me. Looking at Turdy too. I knew she finally remembered me when her expression got suddenly furious and she let a screech out of her. She snatched up her youngest child, who was crawling round her skirts, and began pushing me towards the front door. I shouted at her to wait a moment, to tell me what had happened, if my family had been in contact with her. She paused for a second, then scuttled into the back, returning with post – two letters – telling me all the while that my stuff was gone, had been gone since the first day I left her home. Someone else was living in my room now. Mrs Afandi had got rid of my things. Had got rid of me. Had wiped me from her mind and her room. And now she was trying to get rid of me from her hallway. Move on. Move away. Out. Out. She had rented out my room to someone else. Someone else was living there. She'd forgotten me. Given my stuff to the police who had come the same day I left to check out the fire and see what happened. *To the police*. Can you believe that? That explains how my parents got the low-down on everything – from the police. Can't go there. Can't go to the police. They must know all about me, they've had my belongings since November. They'd catch Turdy. What'll I do? What'll I do?

I sat and tried to think. Sat with Turdy in MacDonald's and smelt the letters. Felt the letters. Stroked them and held them and rocked with them. Comforting. The writing on one was scrawly and sloping and sloppy. It was stamped with an English postmark. The date wasn't readable, but judging by the stains on the envelope and the coffee-ring, Mrs Afandi had had it for some time. The flap was sealed down and I opened it slowly, peering in while Turdy waited. In the end, I pulled the letter out really quickly and opened it up.

It was from Flea. From *Flea*. I can't believe it? All this time he's OK. He's alive. The knife didn't kill him. Graffiti didn't kill him. He's fine. He's better. He's not dead. He's well and all healed up. I read the rest of his letter.

His friends brought him to the hospital where he was stitched up and fixed up and made better. He's left London. Moved up north. He wrote a phone number on the letter and wants me to ring it. Said he'd like to hear from me. He said Graffiti's moved away too – scarpered out of London almost immediately as the police were after him for arson and malicious damage. He won't be back, he said. Won't be looking for me anymore. "Chill out," he said before signing off.

So now I know.

Now I don't have to run.

I can chill out.

I can be proud.

I have survived.

Can you imagine that? All this time I've been running around like some headless chicken scared of Graffiti with his knife, while he's been living the good life in some other smelly city in England a million, billion miles away from me. I've been making him haunt my dreams and spook my days, what with believing I see him everywhere. And it's not him at all! The guy in the station and the old man who left money and Pop-eye and even Turdy never, ever worked for him. Probably never, ever even heard of him. It was all just me. Scaredy old me, making up ghost stories to keep me awake at night.

But now I know. Now I know that Flea's all right and I'm all right. Now I can relax and chill out.

The other letter was one I wasn't opening for a while. The writing was familiar, neat and in block capitals, the envelope pale blue, the postmark Dublin. It was from Clem and I tucked it into my jacket pocket to read some other time.

December 31

We're at the office where Turdy's social worker is based, and she's talking to Turdy in the little back office. It's lashing rain outside and my denim jacket is hanging on the radiator drying because it got drenched. The stink in the room from the drying denim is something else! I'm glad we decided to come here today because the weather's really turned nasty. It was fine for the past couple of days, but now it's blowing some kind of a gale.

I've read Clem's letter. I've read it and read it and

read it so that it already looks like I've had it for about five years, even though I've only had it for two days. It's all blotched and creased and crumpled and smeared and stained. He wrote it way before my phone call on Christmas day.

Clem's well. They're all well. But his letter is dead. Dry. Not Clem-like at all. Just statements and questions. No pleading. No emotion. No anger. No delight about getting my address. Nothing. I don't know what I expected, really. I mean, how much emotion can you put into a letter to someone who's walked out on you and made no contact for four months? And how much can you write when you don't know who's going to read the letter and when?

Perhaps it's me who's dead, dried-up and dead inside like I thought Turdy was when I first saw her. Clem wants to know where I am in London as he knows I've gone from the address he's writing to. He asks question upon question and really gives me the third degree – all the same old stuff they were checking out on the phone like where I am and who I'm with and how I'm managing. But he doesn't tell me that much, just that everyone's fine and to please ring or write or return.

It's good to read the letter, though. Good to hear a voice from home. But funny too. Funny-peculiar that is. It's like being on a ship for days and days and then, when you get off, the solid ground feels odd for a bit. Takes a while to get used to. Perhaps I've been on a ship for weeks and weeks, rocking and rolling and swaying around and now I'm stepping back on solid ground. It'll take a bit for me to get used to the steadiness. I've got my sea legs now. I'm able to take the swaying, the rocking. I can react to it and stay standing. At times I even like it.

Turdy's social worker came out then and asked to talk to me. Turdy sat down and I went into the back office. I didn't know what she wanted, as after all, she's not my social worker and has nothing to do with me. But she had a lot to say to me – stuff I never expected, about Turdy feeling that I helped get her through a really tough time, and that Rosie in the Project told her I was great at talking to other people staying there and listening to them. I was getting more and more embarrassed. Anyway, she finally finished up by asking me if I'd ever thought of working with homeless people, in a shelter or on the streets – especially seeing as I had experience of living rough and it would be a great asset to me! Wow! I just didn't know what to say. Me? Good at this kind of thing? It certainly gave me something to think about.

January 1

New Year's Day! We're in this place called "Caritas House" which is for teenagers who are in-between running away and returning home. There are three others in the house, but they're around somewhere else. I had a long bath this morning and washed my hair. I laundered my jeans and shirt. It's a good feeling to put on clean clothes after a long soak in the bath. I think skin is made for being soaped and washed and then caressed by sweet-smelling cotton, but only when staying indoors.

Grime and sweat and body oils and dried rain and city streets leave an itchiness on your skin that you don't notice so much when you're outside and breeze-blown and walking around – it's like a coating, a natural layer of protection – but once you come indoors for a while, warmth and dryness make you itch and feel hot and uncomfortable. I think I like both sensations – being indoors and fresh *and* being outdoors and layered. They're both the way you're *supposed* to feel in the different habitats.

There's a huge Christmas tree in the corner of the room, so that everywhere smells of pine needles. Turdy will be staying here a while until the social worker finds someplace else for her that'll suit her and she'll settle in – she's not going home to her folks.

I'm not so sure yet about me – not because I'm waiting for the social worker to find somewhere, but because I'm waiting to see what I want to do. It's taking a while for the answer to come to me. My mind, which is trying to decide, is like a separate part of me. It's thinking through all the options and balancing up all the choices. Sometimes I wake up and want terribly to be at home, to be part of the family and be able to get on with them all, and that wish stays with me all day. It would be nice to see everyone again. To spend some time with Mum and Dad. To ring school-friends and see what they're up to. To warm my hands on my family's reactions and to test my own responses.

But sometimes I wake up and want to spend more and more time wandering and ambling on my own and choosing from day to day what I'll do. I like what I'm doing now. Graffiti's gone, so I don't have to hide any more. Flea's alive, so I don't have to worry any more. I *like* being outdoors when it's fresh and bright and sunny.

And I like staying indoors in the hostels when the rain falls and the winds whips up. I liked being in the house for a few days with Mickey, Sattar and Pop-eye. I think, most of all, I like choosing if I want to be indoors or outdoors, whether I want to sleep in or out, whether I want to let my body build up its own layer of oil and sweat and grease, or whether I want to wash it all off.

And I like waiting for my mind to decide what it wants to do, to make the right decisions for me. I'm the subject of its decisions and the slave of its wishes, but I am separate, apart. My mind will decide for me; I must wait and see what it wants. Either way, I'll go along with it and be quite happy in the end.

PART THREE

The sea was choppy and steel-blue. Cold-looking. Sarah wanted to stay out on deck however, where the spray left a salt taste on her lips and the breeze whipped through her hair and freshened her. They were well out of sight of the coast of Wales now, but not yet within view of Ireland. A huge stretch of cold sea, empty of land – just miles and miles of green water that shrank back from the steep steel sides of the ship, sucked by some invisible force, and then reached forwards again in dark, angry waves topped with flecks of creamy foam. The constant movement, threatening at times, gentle and soothing at others, was fascinating to watch. Sarah leaned right over the barrier to see where the bow of the ship cut through the waves, crossing them at an angle and smashing them into smaller waves that fizzled and spat and crashed against the hollow hull furiously. Several times, the ferry passed by other ships crossing the channel – passenger liners and fishing boats, small motor vessels and long sailboats with their tall sails swelling in front of the wind. But for the most part, they were solitary and alone.

Sarah wasn't the only one out on deck. Lots of other passengers preferred to be outdoors too. One man was even bravely attempting to read the newspaper in the stiff breeze. It was a bit much, thought Sarah as she looked at him, given the stiff breeze and coldness. It was hardly as if they were cruising on the *QE2* around the Pacific where it would have been lovely to sit out in the sunshine and browse through a paper. He sat on a wooden bench with a firm grip of his *Times*, his clenched fingers almost blue with the cold. The corners of the pages riffled loudly and sometimes snapped sharply if the wind gusted suddenly, but he wasn't going to be beaten. Hang on he did; how much reading he got done was another matter.

Another man was out with his son, who was no more than seven or eight years of age. The little lad wore short trousers, his mottled legs covered in goose-pimples. His dad had a tight hold of him that no sudden breeze was going to break and, together, they trotted unsteadily around the deck, watching the screaming seagulls that hovered effortlessly above the ship and spotting other boats and ships. Every so often, his dad would point out some new sight to him and the child would turn a pinched face obediently in the direction of his father's pointed hand, shivering as he did so. For heaven's sake, thought Sarah, bring the child indoors before he gets frostbite.

While it was refreshing outside, Sarah herself got cold every so often, even though she was more warmly clad than the wretched child. Then she'd go inside, hauling open the heavy steel-reinforced door and stepping over the steep step, to where it was warm and carpeted. She'd sit with her back against one of the walls and her legs stretched out, looking around at the other passengers and the activity inside the ship until she got warm again. As soon as that happened, it was off outside again because she couldn't stand it inside for too long. For a start, there was awful, gooey piped music played throughout the ship. It was the kind of music you hear in supermarkets or pubs during the daytime – all empty, light and airy. Sarah reckoned it was just played to fill up empty spaces in conversations and to avoid total silence, but it was terrible.

Secondly, there were crowds and crowds of people all over the place. They were queuing up for their duty-free with steel shopping baskets crammed full of bottles of spirits and wines and cigarettes and perfumes. They were sitting in the pullman seats with prams and push-chairs blocking the walkways and babies and dribbling toddlers crawling all over the place and little children playing chasing and hide-and-seek. There were people queuing up for the restaurant and self-service café with trays full of sausages and beans or chips and peas. To make matters worse, there was some kind of school group returning from a trip away and everywhere Sarah looked, she could see gangs of schoolkids in green uniforms and striped ties charging excitedly around the place, trying out the one-armed bandits and fruit machines, gathering in knots at the top and the bottom and the middle of the stairs and racing everywhere they could race without being stopped.

Was there no end to people and more people and even more people around everywhere? Sarah had hoped it was the one thing she'd left behind when she left London. Now here she was, almost back in Ireland and masses of people seemed to be following her. They were spilling out of the confines of London and moving in great shouting, running, noisy waves towards Ireland. Horror of horrors, thought Sarah, she was like some cursed Piper of Hamelin leading them all home.

At least out on deck there were fewer of them.

They were due to dock in Dún Laoghaire at three o'clock that afternoon. Another hour to go, she realised as she checked her watch. Possibly the longest hour she'd spend in a while. Absentmindedly, Sarah began chewing at her fingernails, thinking about her impending arrival home. She wasn't sure if there'd be anyone to meet her at the terminal when she disembarked, and she told herself that she didn't really care whether there was or not. She had managed on her own for the last five months in a strange city, so she was sure she could manage to make her own way home from the ferry in Dún Laoghaire. Her whole family could stay at home and watch telly, or cut the grass, or wash their hair for all she cared. In fact, she'd probably have an easier time of it if she got the bus or train home herself. Then there'd be no awkward hellos and difficult greetings, no uncertainties about whether or not to hug them, or shake their hands, or stand around embarrassingly not knowing what to do.

This is what she'd told herself, and had almost managed to believe it, but really she hoped fervently that she *would* be met. Deep down, she hoped somebody still thought enough about her to want to meet her, to want her to be home, to want her around. Making her lonely way home in her own city where there were many, many people she knew but none of them who wanted to meet her after five months of being away would be far, far more difficult than surviving in the strange streets of London.

She'd been on the phone several times to her parents from Caritas House, talking to them and telling them that she was coming home, that she was getting the ferry, but they had been difficult conversations. She had been straining her ears as she had spoken, trying hard to hear her parents' silent reactions over the static of the long-distance call, trying to sense their feelings across the miles, but it was so frustrating because of the restrictions of the telephone as a way of communicating. She could only hear their words, could only listen to the intonation of their voices, and guess at the silences and the pauses in between. She missed out on the myriad of other ways of listening and hearing when face to face with someone. She was unable to read their expressions – to see if her mother was pursing her lips in disapproval or smiling at her encouragingly. She couldn't tell if her father had his eyebrows raised in sad disappointment or his glasses lifted in surprised delight. She couldn't see how they sat when talking to her, how they rested, how their bodies were. Was her father relaxed and easy in his armchair, or sitting tensely balanced on the edge? Was her mother standing at the kitchen door smiling gently and smoothing the creases in her skirt as she always did when Sarah was talking to her earnestly? Or was she perched on the bottom step of the stairs where she sat when taking serious news on the phone? She missed out on the silent innuendo that passed between her parents when they glanced knowingly at each other – one quick look conveying so much.

If only she could have seen them at the same time, if only she could have smelt and felt and seen and touched them, she would have better understood their emotions, she would have been better able to gauge the reaction that was facing her today. She could hazard a vague guess at it, but their conversations – so difficult to interpret fully – had been guarded, punctuated with many long silences and occasional sighs. They were all so reserved with each other, lacking in enthusiasm and encouragement.

Disappointing.

"So, you've decided to come home, then?"

Her mother. Voice flat. Barely a question, more of a statement. Followed by a sigh. Was this her mother at all?

"Yes . . . " Careful, Sarah. Don't commit yourself to anything you may regret. Be cautious, then you won't have to go back on your word. " . . . for the time being."

Long silence. Quiet cough. Her father this time, on the extension upstairs, introducing himself discreetly.

"Just for the time being then, Sarah?"

"Well, I'll see." What a lousy response, Sarah. Can't you be a little more giving? Don't begrudge them everything. "I might stay . . . I just don't know yet."

Long silence, then her father and mother try to talk at the same time. Difficult to hear. Apologies. Embarrassed pauses.

"Oh, sorry, I thought you were finished."

"You go ahead."

"No, no. After you."

"OK, so. Thanks."

Her mother again.

"So why are you bothering to come home if you may just leave again?"

Quick twist of the knife there. Just a little turn, fast, deadly. Can't let you away with anything, Sarah, can she? Sarcasm. A defence.

"I just want to see you. Just want to spend a bit of

time at home. Is that OK?" Don't lose your patience. Stay calm, cool. They've been through a hard time. Easy, easy. "I thought it would be good – you know. It would help things."

Incoherent grunt. From who – Mum? Dad? What did it mean? Ask them. "Pardon? What did you say?"

Silence. Ask again, don't just let it go. "Did you say something?"

Dad this time.

"So, when are you coming?"

And so it went on. She knew things weren't going to be easy. Not after five months. It would take time. Time for everything to settle – if they settled at all, that is. Would Sarah have the patience to give things time? Had she the interest even? The stamina? At times, she couldn't be bothered with all the effort that would be required. It would be ages, forever, perhaps never, before they felt anyway comfortable with each other again. Things would have changed, relationships dislocated, loyalties shifted.

Sarah felt as though she was preparing to step into quicksand where nothing was certain and everything was moving, changing, shifting. Maybe they would never be the same with each other again. Perhaps the changes were permanent. It was a thought that was both reassuring and frightening. One part of Sarah didn't want her family and her home to be the very same as it had been when she had left. After all, hadn't she left because she wasn't happy with the way things were? Hadn't she left because she couldn't feel a part of her family, because she couldn't relate to them, didn't seem to share the same values as them? There was no point in leaving for several months and then returning to the *status quo* where all was as before. Sarah knew she wouldn't be able to tolerate that. She wouldn't be able to stay for long if everything settled into the same old routine.

But then another part of her, a little voice inside of her, kept worrying about what would have changed. *The devil you know is better than the one you don't* and all that jazz kept running and running around in her mind. Would things be so different that she might not be able to stay, that she was now an outsider, an intruder? The whole family might be working so well together without her around that she might now be a useless piece of baggage, capable only of unsteadying their even keel. Sarah had always been the fly in the ointment at home, the black sheep, the difficult one. She had been the catalyst instrumenting recent events and now she was returning to view her own handiwork, to see the changes she had effected. Her leaving may have been for the better – clearing out the dead wood, so to speak. She shuddered at the thought of it. Of returning home to where she was no longer really wanted, to where she would be the destabilising influence once again.

"Are you all right, miss? Feeling sick or something?" An acne-faced schoolboy in a green uniform leaned towards her on the deck. Sarah blinked, suddenly wakened from her daydreams. Beyond the boy, she could see some of his friends standing close by, watching her curiously. She stood up from where she was sitting on the rusty steps leading to the upper deck, slipping slightly on the wet surface as she did so.

He asked again, eyes concerned.

"You sure you're all right? Not feeling bad with the swaying and all that?"

"I'm fine. Thanks."

They moved off, glancing back at her now and then.

Time to head inside again, Sarah thought, tucking her cold hands into her armpits to stay warm. She'd been sitting out for some time now and was cold. The sky was cloudy, rain threatening. Sarah went indoors, checking her watch again.

Thirty-five minutes to go.

The ferry had been sitting out beyond the harbour for a good twenty minutes, waiting for some little, battered fishing boat to finish unloading its cargo of silvery fish and scuttling crabs and to clear the entrance. Clem had been watching the manoeuvres from the end of the old pier, perched as he was on top of the moss-laden wall.

Waves generated by the reverse thrust of the ferry's engines slapped noisily against the side of the pier, throwing up showers of spray that occasionally splashed against his left shoe. Idly, Clem watched the individual bubbles of spray sit for a moment on the leather and then slowly seep into it, bleeding a little to the left and right as they soaked into the material.

As soon as the fishing boat had moved off again, the ferry slid slowly towards the mouth of the harbour, aligning itself carefully to fit between the old and new piers. At the same time, Clem left the old pier to give himself enough time to get round to the terminal building before the passengers disembarked. Considering that Sarah wasn't sure who was going to pick her up, it was essential that he was there on time, and easily seen.

There were already lots of people gathered at the exit gate to collect family and friends. There were also plenty of curious passers-by watching the impressive vessel pull up alongside the quay.

As he approached the terminal, Clem could see Lee standing next to his dad just outside the main entrance. They had decided to stay there when Clem walked down the old pier. Lee was staring at the huge hull of the ship that now towered way above them. The reverse engines were on again to slow down the massive hulk and they churned up gallons of foaming, weedy seawater that cascaded over the edge of the sea wall and poured on to the concrete walkway. Lee watched in awe, stepping cautiously nearer his father.

Clem was pleased that Lee and his father had wanted to come with him to meet Sarah. Mal had gone to a swimming gala in Limerick that morning and wouldn't be back until late. Clem suspected that it had been orchestrated to avoid his having to face Sarah until he really had to, but he said nothing. It was probably best for Mal as well as for Sarah that he wasn't around for a while.

Alice had decided to stay at home with their mother, who was up to ninety and alternated between being excited about Sarah returning and being furious at herself for getting excited. She had left the house early that morning, saying that she'd be gone for the day. Clem and his father had got concerned as she had told none of them where she was going. Just before two o'clock, however, she returned.

"I couldn't just stay away, could I?" she demanded of them petulantly. "It's only right that I'm here when she gets back."

"Of course it is, love," said Mr Bailey soothingly. "I'll go and collect her and you stay here and get yourself ready."

"I didn't want to be here, you know. I didn't want to be around today, but I couldn't stay away. What would people think? But she doesn't deserve it. She has to learn that not everybody's going to jump on cue merely because she's coming home."

"I'll help calm her down," offered Alice, pulling out one of her bottles of essential oils and lighting up an oil-burner in the kitchen. "I'll stay here with mum. You and Clem and Lee go and collect Sarah."

The front of the ship swung open gradually and the first of the cars and trucks pulled out of the bowels of the ship and drove on to the mainland. A cloud of oily diesel fumes accompanied the first few vehicles.

There was no sign of Sarah. Anxiously, Clem scanned the passengers proceeding down the gangway towards the passenger terminal. Lee and his father did likewise, stepping forwards to see better, although a few feet made no difference.

Then Clem spotted somebody coming towards them, someone who had broken away from the milling crowds. Somebody who was suddenly only a few feet away and approaching confidently. Somebody who wore faded jeans and a oversized jacket, who travelled light with a small sports bag thrown over one shoulder.

He hadn't noticed her until that moment, hadn't been aware of her approach. Perhaps it was a case of his not having recognised her. The stride was familiar, the lift of the head and the erect carriage were too, but after that Clem hesitated. Was this Sarah? Was this his sister with whom he had shared most of his life?

She was thinner than he remembered – too thin now for her height – and had a tanned face. Her hair was cropped short, emphasising her bone structure, initially severe but pleasing once he got used to it. Gone were the long curls that softened her face, the plumpness of her cheeks that gave her the look of a little girl. Clem blinked in surprise, slightly put out by the physical changes. He smiled and immediately moved to embrace her, an automatic reaction that she obviously hadn't anticipated. He felt her angular frame stiffen slightly from his hug, then relax and return the warmth of his welcome. He knew she must feel uncomfortable, knew she was putting great effort into her casual stride and easy smile. He could sense the hesitation in her touch, could see the doubt in her eyes.

Clem had established the warmth of the welcome and the others followed suit, Lee jumping up to Sarah, although he found to his surprise that he didn't have to jump quite so far as he remembered to kiss her. Her father moved to take her bag, but Sarah refused, smiling shyly at him and maintaining a firm grip on it.

Clem talked little in the car on the way home, preferring to watch his sister, to observe the changes in her. He sat in the back seat with Lee, while she occupied the passenger seat next to her father and they talked innocuously of Dublin and the weather and her journey home. Time enough for more difficult talks later on, and everyone was silently aware of that, pleased to start off with safe subjects.

Sarah's mannerisms were sometimes the same as Clem recalled, sometimes different. She had a new way of snatching a glimpse of something – something perhaps outside the car window, or a movement of Lee's. She'd glance swiftly at it, taking it in, not missing a jot yet maintaining the flow of the conversation. She also used her hands more in speech, sketching her descriptions in the air in a way that reminded Clem of Alice, yet was also uniquely Sarah. She dipped and flickered her fingers, stirring currents of air and adding a richness to her talk.

Sarah, too, observed and took in all she saw, although it was harder for her as there were so many questions asked of her and so much more input expected from her. She appreciated their coming to collect her, guessing at the angst and tensions in the house before her ship was due to dock. She knew it was important to talk easily so that everybody felt secure and relaxed and so she looked with interest at the changes in the city that her father pointed out to her as they drove through – the new office block on the corner of the square, the rows of daffodils along the centre of the dual carriageway. She noticed too the extra few inches that Lee had grown; the curious, questioning glances of Clem; the hesitant way her father held the car door open for her, not sure of her reaction. These first few moments were the most important as they would be the ones that she and her family would remember tonight and tomorrow and next week.

The hilltop was breezy and cold. All around, at ankle level, fraughan blossoms grew in profusion, little blushing flowers that sent up clouds of sweet-smelling pollen as she walked. Sarah breathed in the scented spring air.

She peered into the wind, squinting against its sharpness to view the terrain ahead. The mountain-top was deceptive. From the ground, it looked like a straightforward mountain with one peak, but once you were up on it, you realised that there were really three small peaks clustered together and that each one had to be climbed separately. Small valleys dipped steeply between each peak.

Sarah paused, breathing heavily and welcoming the cold wind on her hot cheeks. Adjusting the straps of her rucksack, she checked her map before stepping out again, beginning to feel the first twinge of protest from her calf muscles. The cairn she was heading for was on the third peak – an ancient man-made depression of stones, rimmed with a circle of larger rocks – the ideal location for a wind-sheltered lunch. They could all snuggle together for protection from the wind and munch their food. Sarah shifted her gaze skywards. Judging by the gathering clouds, there was perhaps an hour or so of dry weather left before the rain set in, so there'd be just enough time to eat a quick sandwich before making for home. They'd been lucky with the weather so far, though. All they'd experienced since setting out a couple of hours ago were a few half-hearted drops of rain that scarcely dampened their jackets or their spirits.

At the top of the second peak, Sarah paused and looked back to see where the others were. Clem and Lee were just descending the side of the first peak, Lee running down it with the careless abandon of a little boy while Clem stepped more carefully, avoiding any moguls or scattered rocks. Lee glanced up and waved at Sarah, then stood waiting impatiently for Clem, hopping from one foot to the other. Sarah smiled to herself. Physically, Lee had changed most during the time she had been in London. He was now almost up to her shoulders, his previously stocky frame leaner.

Everyone else had changed too, but not physically. The changes in them were not immediately apparant but only surfaced after weeks of being home again, after the newness of being back had worn off, after the gloss of polite reserve had been rubbed away by old familiarity and customary conversations.

In the beginning, immediately after her return, everyone was careful with what they said, how they reacted. They were all polite and awkwardly friendly until routines had been established again. It was as if they were all stepping in and out of a formal dance where the movements and steps were written in stone and couldn't be altered until a certain amount of time had elapsed. No one put a foot wrong. They played expertly by the rules, taking time to listen and to then contribute, to ask questions with sensitivity and reply with care. Sarah too had played by the rules, knowing that it was only when they relaxed that the true emotions and feelings would spill out. It had been weeks before Sarah could read the changes that had occured in everyone. None of them spoke directly about the time she had been away, about how they had felt and what they had done. It was carefully avoided as a subject, apart from the occasional sarcastic comment by Mal or her mother, or Lee's disarming directness.

Gradually, she learned of their reactions by their way of addressing her now. Piece by piece, little by little, she built up a picture of how things had been for them. It was as if she was doing a large and complicated jigsaw in her head, made up of her family's feelings and emotions and comments. Some pieces would always remain missing, while others were there for the choosing from the very beginning. Like, for example, Lee's utter openness. Being the youngest, he was less inhibited by social graces and therefore it was easiest to answer his direct questions. He also wanted to spend most of this free time with Sarah, going to the shops and swimming and getting the bus into town with her. Perhaps it was an indication of how much he had missed being with her.

"Sarah," he asked when the two of them were walking to the library. "Were you happy when you ran away?"

"Sometimes I was, Lee, and at other times, I was very unhappy and lonely."

"I was unhappy when you were away. I missed you. Why didn't you come home when you were lonely?"

"It's not always the best thing to do what you want as soon as you want it. Sometimes it's better to try and work through something yourself."

"Will you run away again?"

Sarah'd smiled at that one. "I don't know."

"Will you bring me with you if you do?"

"You're a bit young for that sort of thing yet, Lee. But I promise that if I leave home again, I'll write to you often."

Her mother's reaction contrasted sharply with Lee's. Rather than let her off to do her own thing, she expected Sarah to take full part in every family event. It was as if she believed that Sarah's return home was an admission that she had been wrong. She seemed to think that Sarah now wanted to be a full member of the family and to play her rightful role as obedient daughter and sister. Therefore, she expected Sarah to be at every meal where they ate *en famille*, to attend Mass with them every Sunday (although Sarah hadn't been to Mass since the previous September), to stay in on Sunday evenings and watch television. Sarah went along with her for the sake of peace, rather than rock the boat immediately after arriving home, but silently she resented this pressure to follow every family routine. She simmered as she sat with her parents and her brothers and sister watching family programmes and regular soaps. She chewed in mute indignation at the dinner table every night, and vowed that this wouldn't go on for much longer. It couldn't – something had to give.

She stepped to one side now and strained to see where Alice was. Further back, she could glimpse the bright pink of her hat bobbing over the top of the peak as she made her slow way up. Her friends Jasmine and Eliza were with her, chatting and meandering through the heather, picking flowers for pressing as they wandered.

Turning towards the cairn again, Sarah moved on, determined to get some lunch for herself before the rain started. Clem looked at her from the first peak, watched her move onwards and away, ever further from them all. Always away from them. This was the new Sarah. The changed Sarah, impatient and unsettled, champing at the bit, restless. She was always eager to do something new, something different. She never lounged around the place or stretched out in front of the telly for the evening. If she was with the family for any length of time, she spent her time watching everyone else in the room instead of the programme on the screen, her eyes flickering around in that new way of hers.

Clem bent down and picked up a smooth round pebble, brushing off the dry clay that stuck to its marbled surface.

"What's that, Clem?" Lee enquired, moving up next to him and reaching over to take the pebble and have a look at it. Clem glanced at his little brother.

"Bet you can't find another one as smooth as it," he challenged him, handing over the little stone. Lee responded immediately to the challenge, scouring the stony path for white, marbled pebbles, running forwards every few moments and pausing to peer at the masses of tiny stones scattered at his feet.

Clem strolled on, filling his lungs with the mountain air and relishing the richness of the view. Glancing up as he reached the summit of the second peak, he was surprised to see Sarah sitting still on a large granite rock. She was gazing out at the blue-hazed view of Wicklow and, beyond, the city of Dublin.

"Isn't this amazing?" she asked, not turning at Clem's approach.

"Mmm," he agreed, squatting beside her.

Lee appeared beside them.

"Bet I'll get to the cairn first," he shouted, charging off with boundless energy.

"Save me the best rock," Sarah shouted after him.

Clem and Sarah stayed where they were a few moments longer and then Sarah stood up. She looked upwards at the grey clouds.

"Come on," she said. "Let's join Lee in the cairn for lunch before the rain sets in for the day. We'll get drenched otherwise."

"Yes," replied Clem, rubbing his stomach thoughtfully. "I'm starving."

Together, they descended the side of the peak, towards where they could see Lee's head over the rim of the cairn. They were not quite comfortable with each other yet and their silence was expectant, awkward, uncomfortable. A lot had been left unsaid between them. A lot of ground had still to be covered.

"What are you going to do with yourself in the autumn?" Clem asked.

Sarah breathed deeply.

"I'm not so sure at the moment. I don't think I want to go back to school, although I could go into fifth year and just skip transition. But the thought of it leaves me cold. Work doesn't sound such a big deal either, though I've been thinking things through a lot lately."

Clem laughed.

"So that leaves staying at home," he remarked lightly.

Sarah glanced at him sharply, suddenly serious.

"Does it? There are plenty of alternatives to that one."

Her words were barbed, her tone defensive. Clem was taken aback by her retort. For one second, for just an instant, he had replied without thinking about what he was going to say and immediately Sarah indicated that he had overstepped the mark. Back in your box, Clem.

"Whoa, Sarah," he said. "Take it easy. I was only teasing."

Sarah said nothing, a silent acknowledgement of his mild reprimand. Clem continued, keeping his voice even.

"Do you think you might leave home again?"

Sarah was quiet for a time. Thinking. When she spoke, she was hesitant, cautious.

"I might. I'm not so sure. It's good to spend some time at home, but I can't really see myself hanging around for long."

When he said nothing, she got courage and spoke with more conviction.

"Let's face it, I don't really fit in at home, Clem. I'm the different one, the odd one out. I sometimes feel I ended up with the wrong family when I was born, mixed up the address I was meant for. There's probably some crackpot family out there somewhere with a level-headed, conservative, studious daughter who's wondering why she doesn't fit in. *I'm* supposed to be part of their lot and *she's* supposed to be a Bailey."

Clem laughed at the image of two dimple-cheeked

infants floating down on little fluffy clouds to two completely different mothers but somehow getting confused on the way and ending up with the wrong families.

"I'm serious, Clem," Sarah continued, grinning at the same time. "I'm different to all of you. And not only that, I don't *want* to be the same. I don't want to try and fit in because being the same as everyone else in the family isn't how I want to be."

Clem was serious again.

"But why are you so against us?"

Sarah looked at him in surprise. "It's not that I'm *against* you, it's just that I don't want the same as you. It's two different things. If you're all happy with yourselves, then that's fine. It's good. But count me out of it. I want to do different things with my life."

"And leaving is the only solution you have?"

She stopped in her tracks and gazed at him. "What do you suggest?" she demanded.

"It depends on what you want to be. You don't have to leave to do whatever you want, you know."

Sarah considered his challenge.

"Maybe I just want to be free to choose myself what I want to be. I'm not saying that the way I lived in London is what I aspire to – it's not, because at times it was awful and dirty and scarey, but at least I was making my own decisions. I was choosing how I wanted to live and I could do whatever I liked."

"But you don't have to leave home to do whatever you like," Clem reiterated.

"Of course I do," Sarah responded immediately. "Can you just see Mum and Dad's faces if I decided not to work or go back to school? They'd go mad – the shame it'd bring on the family and all that. I'd never hear the end of it."

They reached the cairn where Lee was busy setting out his sandwiches and opening his flask.

"I don't know," Clem said. "Is it any worse than leaving home and living like a down-and-out in London?"

Sarah ignored his comment and hopped down into the cairn beside Lee. They busied themselves with unpacking sandwiches and opening flasks, trying to ignore the awkward, angry silence that had settled over them yet again.

That night, Sarah lay in bed, wide awake. It was after two and the house was silent. Sometimes, cars drove along the dark street outside and she idly watched the reflection of their lights slide across the ceiling. She'd been awake for several hours, since first going to bed, in fact, as sleep had never really caught up with her. Her body was still, but her mind was vivid with thoughts and ideas and notions that swirled around madly, jumbled together in baffling chaos.

Her thoughts had been like that for several days now, confused and complicated. It worried her when she got like this. She knew she wasn't settled or comfortable with being home or relaxed. She could feel a sense of frustration building uncontrollably in her body and mind. She had no command over it. Its insistence disturbed her. She knew that eventually she would have to respond to it, to react to it, to do something. She was genuinely trying to settle at home, trying to conform to her family's ways that were as familiar to her as they were frustrating, but she knew deep down that she was fighting a losing battle. Her feet itched to move on. Her mind constantly recalled the good times she had had when away from her family, the benefits of living a free and easy existence without the binds of parental expectations and the rigours of structures and routines.

She'd written to Turdy in Caritas House several times since coming home and had received back two crazy letters that made virtually no sense, so Sarah learned little of what was happening for Turdy. Sarah missed her and longed to talk to her, to find out how things had worked out with the social worker, to see where she was going to live and what was happening to her mother and her mother's boyfriend. She missed wandering round with Turdy, doing as they pleased, window-shopping and rat-riding, staying in the *Jerusalem Cold Weather Project* or in Pop-eye's dilapidated house.

She'd also written to Bakhtiar, but not surprisingly, had received no response. Neither had she managed to get an answer when she rang the phone number Flea had written down for her. She was anxious to establish some contact with the people she had met in London and, despite her efforts, had not received any positive reponses.

Equally, home was increasingly restrictive for her. Her mother's insistence on her taking part in every family occasion was by now rubbing on raw nerves for Sarah. Mild protestations fell on deaf ears and Sarah was reluctant to start World War III with an all-out confrontation. She guessed it was difficult for her mother, who was trying to make Sarah feel welcome in the only way she knew how, which was to include her in everything, to tell her frequently how much she enjoyed having her around, how much she had missed her presence. At times, however, Sarah thought her mother's words sounded as if they were said through gritted teeth, but she appreciated the effort.

And her father was so worried that she might run away again that he liked to know her every movement: where she was and who she was with, how long she was likely to be and when she planned to get home. Whenever possible, he collected her in the car so that she felt like a small child again. And although she loved Lee dearly, she was getting a little tired of his wanting to go everywhere with her. This was so different from the utter freedom that she had enjoyed in London.

Even with her friends, she was now an outsider. Karen was full of talk about her new boyfriend, about the transition year in school and what they had done on it. Sarah could only talk of London and living in hostels and on the streets, of working and earning a living and of budgeting on a limited income. Sarah found they had little in common other than their pasts, but there wasn't much in a conversation that dredged up old memories from almost a year ago.

She read and reread her diary from the days when Graffiti had frightened her out of the Afandi house. She tried to recreate in her mind the fear and terror she had felt then, as a salve to her restless thoughts. She decided that if she was able to truly recall her alarm, it would make the sanctuary of her home appear more appealing.

But it didn't work.

Rather than feel happier, she only got more restless, yearning for excitement, for change, for anything but the tedium of her day, the routine pariticpation in family life that was boring, boring, boring.

Sarah knew she couldn't stick things for much longer.

Epilogue

The spring morning was bright and clear as Sarah quietly shut the front door behind her. She turned towards the gate and breathed in the freshness, her step light despite the heavy bag slung across her shoulder. There was a perfume on the dawn breeze, untainted yet by the fumes and pollution of city life, and, with a thrill of excitement, Sarah believed she could even smell the salt of the sea above the high, sweet notes of blossom fragrance. The street was empty and her footsteps echoed in the stillness.

Looking towards the sky, Sarah saw only a few streaky clouds on the horizon. The day promised fine. The forecast had been good. It would be an easy crossing on the ferry, she decided as she made her way towards Dún Laoghaire, towards the docks. She was neither happy nor sad to be leaving her family again. It just was. It had to be done. She had no choice. She needed to move on and away.

But this time, it was different. This time, inside her,

nestling in the back of her mind, Sarah had a goal, a plan that was still vague and ill-formed – but it was there nevertheless. Months ago, in the small back office in the premises of the social services, an idea had been seeded by a social worker who had spoken unexpectedly to Sarah. Sarah had nurtured her idea and had pondered long and hard on the social worker's words. Would she, Sarah, not think of working with homeless people, in a shelter or on the streets? Would she? Would she? It sounded challenging and real and so . . . so . . . so *her* that Sarah knew that she would love it. Sarah had been good at helping her friend Turdy, she had enjoyed listening to the others who stayed in the Cold Weather Project and knew that they liked talking to her about themselves and their lives. She had experience of living on the streets, frightening and dirty and cold as they were, which made it easier to empathise with and understand their fears. Maybe this, then, was her place, her niche. Working with others living on the streets, particularly if she had some real way of helping them, some way of making things a bit better for them, sounded a great way to work – if she was suited to it. There was only one way Sarah would truly find that out, and that was to live her goal and discover it for herself. She planned to return to the Project and talk to Rosie, to seek out Turdy and talk to her, to meet with her social worker and ask her advice. Then, only then, would her vague ideas crystallise and become clear to her, so that Sarah would understand them and could do something positive about them.

Behind her, Sarah left what she believed to be a

sleeping household. Her carefully worded note lay innocently on the kitchen table beneath the marmalade jar where she knew Mal would be the first to find it when he came down to breakfast before leaving to train the junior swimmers in the swimming club. Once again, it was probably inadequate in expressing her feelings and her great need to leave, but Sarah had long ago decided that all such notes were inadequate.

As she turned the corner at the end of the road without once looking back at her home for the past sixteen years, Sarah was unaware of Clem watching her from the front bedroom window. He watched her disappear around the corner, leaning his forehead against the cold glass as he did so, a white circular smudge on the glass bluring his clear view of his sister before she finally vanished from sight.

He had known it was coming to this. He had known for weeks that Sarah was leaving again – perhaps even before she knew for certain herself. He could feel the energy build in her as she prepared to leave, and this morning he was awake early, listening for her first stirrings.

But he stayed in his bed as she prepared to depart.

He didn't go out to her.

He didn't want to talk to her, to say goodbye, to tell her how much he'd miss her and how much he would have liked her to stay. He knew his words would have little effect except to make her leaving all the harder. She had to go and he had to respect that.

Sarah was made for a life different from his, and, when she was ready, she'd contact him again.

Look for other BEACON BOOKS
published by Poolbeg

*"Literary books for discriminating
young adult readers"*

❧

The Song of the River by Soinbhe Lally

Charlie's Story by Maeve Friel

Circling the Triangle by Margrit Cruickshank

The Homesick Garden by Kate Cruise O'Brien

When Stars Stop Spinning by Jane Mitchell

Shadow Boxer by Chris Lynch

Different Lives by Jane Mitchell

Ecstasy and other stories by Ré Ó Laighléis

❧

BEACON BOOKS